ALL IN THE
MIND

PAUL FERRAR

**To find out more about this book
or to contact the author, please visit:
www.vividpublishing.com.au /allinthemind**

Copyright © 2023 Paul Ferrar

ISBN: 978-1-922788-71-9
Published by Vivid Publishing
A division of Fontaine Publishing Group
P.O. Box 948, Fremantle
Western Australia 6959
www.vividpublishing.com.au

A catalogue record for this
book is available from the
National Library of Australia

This book was written on Ngunnawal land
and the author acknowledges its people as
the traditional owners of the land

For F.

R.I.P.

It's all in the mind, you know....

> Catchphrase spoken
> by Wallace Greenslade,
> *The Goon Show*,
> BBC Radio, 1951-1960

There's nowt as queer as folk....

> Old North Country English saying

All the world's mad but thee and me,
and thee's a bit queer

> Old Yorkshire saying

PROLOGUE
LANCASTER, NW ENGLAND

The small figure was moving quickly, not quite slinking but trying to be unobtrusive. There was only the faintest moonlight, which helped. Not that there were many people to see her, at 10.40 at night. Scattered windows were still lit, but they were curtained to hide the hobbies, obsessions, insomnia or sex that were going on inside.

She was ashamed at what she was going to do. Ashamed not just at the act, but at the fact that she hadn't yet had the courage to end it. Angry also at the circumstances that had given other people power over her – over what she could be made to do. The events from the hospital. The earlier events after the trial, and then the awful people who'd menaced her, pursued her and later threatened to expose her and her past.

But she had a possibility of a new and better job coming, and she needed to move on now. Perhaps tonight could be the end of at least some of it. She'd tell him that tonight was the last time. And if he threatened her further she could also retaliate by saying that she'd expose him too. She didn't think he'd like that.

She had a weapon with her this time for protection, too. A small but sharp knife, though she hoped it wouldn't be needed.

She walked quickly along the footpath, which after a while ran beside a long and high stone wall. Large stones, sandy-yellow and mottled with lichen, moss and a general patina of old age.

After several hundred yards she came to a wooden door in the wall. She glanced quickly around, then tried the handle to see if it opened. It would normally have been bolted, but tonight it was unlocked. He'd undone it – he was obviously expecting her. She slipped through the archway and re-bolted the door.

Inside the wall it was dark among the many trees. Tall, old elms and chestnuts arched towards each other to screen out what faint moonlight there was, and there were no lights shining on the gravel path. However, she knew the path so well that she could hurry towards the hulk of the building ahead of her without missing a step.

And she was so sure there would be nobody in the grounds at that time of night that she didn't see a small, bent figure, motionless in the shadow of a large elm tree. But the watcher saw her, and knew.

This was the night – the night when it would all finally end.

As indeed it did…

SHARON JOHNSON

The disco isn't that good really. Dunno why I bother to come. The guys are all creeps. They only want to get their hands on you. All over you.

The music isn't great either. Well, the music's okay, but the deejay's crap. Trying to sound American and just sounding phony. Thinks he's an FM-pop presenter, but he's just a little sales clerk. Where I work, actually. He thinks he's great but he's shit really. He only gets to do the disco because his dad pays for the hall.

I was thinking of fading when I heard this voice behind me.

'Well, who's this nice wee lassie here?'

Jimmy McTavish. Lancaster's Scottish hunk. That sexy Scottish accent. That body.

He ripples a few muscles at me. My heart skips a few beats, and keeps skipping. Everybody wants to be noticed by Jimmy. This'll show the girls. Pity that slag Shirley isn't here to see. I'll tell her anyway.

We dance for a bit, then Jimmy says:

'I was thinkin' of goin' home a bit early tonight. Maybe stoppin' off along the way. Would you like me to walk you home? The streets are no' so safe these days.'

I can't speak. Every girl wants to be where I am now, and I can't find a word. I just nod.

It's not that early anyway. Nearly three o'clock.

We set off arm in arm. I know inside of me what's going to happen, but I don't care. Well, I don't know if I do care or not, but I haven't got much choice now. The choice was back at the disco. If there was a choice even there.

Maybe it won't happen. Maybe what they say about Jimmy isn't all true.

Jimmy says: 'Why don't we take the short cut along the railway line?'

What they say is definitely true, then.

We go down the steps at the bridge and start walking along the edge of the track. I hope no trains come. There's no moon and it's really dark – you can hardly see the path to walk on. I have to hang on to Jimmy to find where I'm going.

Short cut's a laugh anyway. Every girl in Lancaster knows the bit between the two bridges is called Shag Alley. There's a flat patch in the bushes about half way between the two bridges. We'll be lucky if it's empty, though Jimmy'd make them move on if there was anyone there. They reckon he's tough, Jimmy.

He slips his hand lower round my waist, and into the top of my pants.

Jimmy's said to have the biggest prick in Lancaster. Okay, the other girls probably make it up a bit, but there must be some truth in it. I don't know what I think about that. Bit excited. Bit afraid. Not that I've got much choice, anyway.

If he's feeling me up I may as well do it back. Check out what the girls say. If they're exaggerating.

But I never do find out. My hand is just going in when Jimmy suddenly stumbles forward and falls. His hand comes out of my pants and mine out of his.

'Wha' the fuck?'

It's really dark, and he has to bend down to see what he's tripped over.

'Fuckin' 'ell! Fuck me! It's a tart! It's a body!'

He bends down further and feels her. 'She's dead. She's cold.'

I scream. Scream and scream, till he tells me to shut the fuck up.

I look then. It's horrible. She's naked, and somebody's put her across the line so her neck's on the rails. Her legs were sticking out across the path, which was why Jimmy'd tripped.

Then we hear the sound of a train coming. Jimmy pulls her head off the track. 'Fuck, we can't leave her like that,' he says. The train roars past – an express goods train so there were no lights.

Then Jimmy says 'You'd better stay here and I'll go and get the police.'

I'm hoping he'll leave her. Someone else might find her then. But I guess we can't do that. What if it'd been my body? I wouldn't want that.

But I'm not staying. 'You can't leave me here, you can't. What if the person that done her in's still here? I'm coming with you. You can't leave me. You can't.'

I wish I'd never agreed to go with Jimmy that night. It done me no good. No good at all.

NEXT MORNING

LANCASTER POLICE HQ

Early on the morning when the body was discovered, Inspector Lewis Brady called a meeting of all available CID personnel. They sat on the uncomfortable chairs in the rather dismal meeting room, and there was a lot of shuffling of feet and chairs. They were a bit thinner on the ground than Brady would have liked, but it would hopefully be enough.

'Right, you'll all have heard about the female deceased who was found along the railway during the night. She was strangled, and scene of crime and forensics are at the site at the moment.

'The location was along the railway track between the Marston Road bridge and the Atherton Road bridge, at the area of flattish and open ground that's known locally as Shag Alley. It's a favourite area for outdoor sex, obviously, and one quite possible scenario is that the victim tried to resist and was strangled, or somebody got far too carried away. So I suggest we pursue that line first, while not counting out any other possibilities.

'We can't inspect the site till the scene of crime people have finished, but we'll get an appeal out through all the usual media for anyone who saw anything unusual or anyone in that area late last night and into early this morning.

'One thing that might help us a bit is that the two people who found her said she was placed so that her neck was across the metal of the railway track, with her head inside the lines and her body outside them. Charming, eh?

'I'm guessing at the moment that was to reduce evidence of the strangulation when a train ran over her, but she was found before a train had done so. She was found about 3.25 this morning, and a goods train passed very soon afterwards. Sergeant Nielsen – you contact the railway people urgently to find out the movements of trains on the southbound track last night. If we can get the time of the previous train it'll narrow down our time frame a hell of a lot.

'I don't think the two who found the body would have had anything else to do with it. James McTavish, more commonly known as Jimmy, is a bit of a lad but he's never been involved with anything like this, and Sharon Johnson isn't known to us at all. They say they were just taking a short cut home, but I'm guessing they were after a quickie on the railway bank. Murder doesn't fit with them, but we'll have to do it right. PC Higgs, would you interview as many people as possible who were at the disco in Strang Street last night. It would have been pretty busy and there should be plenty who'd remember McTavish – he's a well-known character locally. Find out what time he might have left. Likewise with Sharon Johnson – she said she goes there regularly and some 'ud remember her. Also check if there's a CCTV.

'The rest of you, I'd like you to get to the site now. As soon as the scene of crime people are out of there you can do a thorough search. You can look around the exact spot in case you can see anything, but they should have done a good job there so you could spend more of your time on the areas alongside the track between the two road bridges. There may not be much sign of anything if she was killed at the spot, but you never know. One thing in particular you could look for is any women's clothing, because she was completely naked and there were no clothes in the immediate area. Her gear might help us to identify her if we're lucky.

'Any questions at this stage?'

PC Garfield spoke up. 'Sir, do you think it might have been one of the loonies? One of the hospitals isn't all that far from there.'

Inspector Brady thought for a rather brief moment, then said: 'Well, we'll have to keep that in mind as a possibility, but I think it's a faint one. I reckon all the patients'd be in their wards at that hour – at least not wandering round the streets killing people. But let's not forget it.

'So, any other thoughts?'

There was the usual murmuring, but no questions.

* * *

They met again at four o'clock that afternoon, and the gloomy faces gave the message before Inspector Brady did. He summed up progress – and mostly the lack of it.

'Len Nielsen's checked with the railway people about trains on the line where she was placed. There was an overnight express from Glasgow that went through at about 1.15 am, and nothing after that until the goods train at 3.25 am that just missed her.

'A preliminary post mortem put her time of death at between ten o'clock last night and midnight, which makes you wonder what was happening with her if she was killed on that spot but not put on the track until half past one or later, but they did say that was only a rough time of death.

'The scene of crime people found bugger all in the area, and forensics haven't come up with anything concrete at this stage. You lot didn't find any clothing anywhere in the vicinity, and we haven't got any ID on the victim at this stage. She doesn't have any tatts on her or any other particular features except a few old scars – probably from cuts – on the back of one hand, and one finger which is slightly crooked.

'The appeal on the media's gone out, but we haven't had any reports of anything in from the public yet. It'll be on the six o'clock news again tonight – if we're lucky that might bring in something.

'PC Higgs – anything from the disco yet?'

'Sir, I found nine different people all of whom swear that McTavish was there all evening, and most thought he left at around three o'clock when things were winding down anyway. They reckoned he was dancing with a nice-looking girl all the time during the second part of the night, and three people knew her as Sharon Johnson. They all said that she and McTavish left together. And to cap that, sir, there was a CCTV and it confirms it all including the time of departure.'

'Good work, Higgs. That does put them out of the picture then. But other than narrowing down the time frame we haven't really got anything yet. Has anybody got anything to add to that rather dismal summary?'

Sergeant Nielsen was the only one to speak up.

'Sir, I was wondering about the discrepancy between the time of death and the placement on the railway line. Could it mean that she was killed somewhere else earlier and then dumped at the railway a bit later?'

'Rather than a bit of nookie at the spot that got out of hand you mean? Yep, that's certainly a possibility. She wasn't all that large a woman so a strong guy could probably carry her, but it would be a bit of an effort to get her down from the bridge and at least several hundred yards along the line. He'd have been lucky not to be seen, too. Though maybe not at two in the morning. Anyway, good point, Len – thank you.

'Anyone else?'

Silence all around, and they agreed to meet at ten the next morning to review further developments.

* * *

At the ten o'clock meeting there was only one other small piece of information that might or might not be relevant. A man who'd seen the appeal for information on the late TV news the previous evening had phoned to say that he'd seen a small white estate car parked off the road – a bit awkwardly – at the Marston Road bridge when he knocked off from stacking supermarket shelves at about two in the morning. He'd assumed it had broken down or run out of petrol or something, or the driver had been drunk and arrested, but he thought it might have been worth mentioning. When he'd driven past next lunchtime it had gone – not that that meant anything.

Inspector Brady said: 'That might back up Len's idea of someone down there dumping the body at that time, though it mightn't either. PC Garfield – would you go through and see how many white estate cars are listed by the car licensing authorities for this general area. If it's not a huge number we might check with their drivers as to what they were doing at that time last night. And you might at the same time check the drunk driving arrests for last night, to see whether the white estate was one of those.

'And we urgently need to get an ID on the victim. PC Robbins – would you put out a missing persons appeal for a woman – probably around forty years old, and about five foot or so in height. Make it national and give it some priority, will you.'

And in the absence of anything else new they had to leave it there.

* * *

It took PC Garfield over a day to run through white estate cars. He reported back to Sergeant Nielsen, and it wasn't all that helpful.

'Sarge, there's around a hundred and forty white estate cars of all makes in a radius of forty miles or so from Lancaster. I can check with their drivers if you like, but it'll take some time.'

'Aye, that's a lot. More than I would have expected. Maybe if you could get it down to those within about ten miles or so and see how many you're left with then. It could be someone from further afield, but it might be a start. You might also like to check with the man who reported the car whether he has the slightest idea of what make of car it was. I don't suppose he got the number plate or he'd have told us, but any comments that might narrow it down a bit would be helpful.'

* * *

PC Garfield came back to the group a day later with thirty-two small white estates within the close Lancaster area. He'd tried to contact all the owners and had – rather surprisingly – got all but three of them. Less surprisingly, they all had alibis or denied that they'd been out that late – they were asleep in bed. Some said that the neighbours ought to be able to testify that their cars were in their driveways at the relevant time of night. Two had been working away from Lancaster that night, confirmed by their employers. One had been working at a night club that was still going at four in the morning. One was part of a small team of office cleaners who worked at night, one was a night watchman at a soft drinks factory, one was a nurse at one of the two local mental hospitals who was on night shift at the time, one was in intensive care in hospital following a heart attack, and one was a porter on night shift at the main infirmary. And all the rest were sleeping the sleep of the innocent, if you believed them.

'Thanks, lads,' said Inspector Brady. 'You've done your best, I know. We're probably not going to get much further until we can get an ID. Let's hope some ray of light shines there soon.'

* * *

A small amount of further information did come in from the final report of the pathologist. The victim had died from strangulation, and the time of death was now more definitely set at between eleven and midnight – probably nearer eleven. In addition to the evidence of strangulation there were also a number of longish and quite deep cuts on the victim's right arm. The pathologist thought that they'd probably been inflicted by a knife.

There were also signs that the victim had had very recent sexual activity, but the person involved must have worn a condom because there were no traces of semen, and no DNA other than the victim's had yet been found. But the other unusual twist was that the pathologist believed that the sexual activity had taken place after death rather than before it.

And there was still no ID for the victim. The case was becoming more baffling as time went on.

THREE WEEKS EARLIER

CHRISTIANE GUCHEZ

I can't remember when I'd had such a bad day.

It started ten minutes after I'd got to work, when the university central computer system crashed. I'm the manager for the system, so I get the blame whether it's my fault or not. I got the main technician in quickly, and he managed to locate the problem – which was a software one – and fix it reasonably fast. However, I knew what the result would be, and it wasn't long before the first calls of complaint came in. Everyone reckoned that their work had been seriously affected – schedules upset, data lost and so on.

As luck would have it, there was one research program that did have a legitimate complaint – their work was just at a critical stage of data manipulation, and they lost a significant amount of work. I did feel bad about that one, even though it wasn't my fault. It's always the centre manager who's caused the problem, regardless.

By the time I got to the canteen at lunchtime, all the palatable food had gone, so I just bought an apple and a banana and went back to make some coffee in the computer centre. And of course the banana turned out to be black down the middle – from the outside it had looked fine.

With all the carry-on I was late leaving, and I missed my usual bus. And the coup de grace for the whole day was when I arrived back at the house, where I have a tiny room, and I was hailed by my landlady, Mrs Marshall.

'Miss Guchez, could I have a word with you, please?'

I've told her to call me Christiane, but she never has. The polite approach was ominous, too.

'I'm sorry to have to do this, but I'll have to ask you to leave here. Something's come up with my daughter, and she needs to find somewhere to live, so I'll have to give her your room.'

I knew perfectly well what would have happened – the daughter will have been thrown out by the no-hoper boyfriend she's been living with. Though that might have a positive side for her too because I think he beats her up.

'I'll have to find somewhere else myself, and you know that's not easy in Lancaster at the moment. What sort of time frame were you thinking of?'

'Well, I'm a fair woman' – that's a laugh – 'and I'll say four weeks' notice.'

She looked slightly relieved – she'd probably expected me to put up more of a fight. I did think of it but I knew it'd be hopeless, and after today I just didn't have the energy. I just contented myself with thinking of her daughter in my shoebox of a room. I'm quite slim and I only just fit – the daughter's grossly fat, and she's going to have a real challenge.

'Okay, Mrs Marshall – I'll start looking for another place tomorrow.'

'Thank you so much, Miss Guchez. My daughter will be very appreciative – she's in the family way at the moment and she doesn't want things to worry about.'

Mon Dieu! The fit's going to be even worse than I thought, and there's no way she'll be able to get a baby in there as well. Not my problem, thank God.

I went upstairs and squeezed myself into the room. I won't miss it at all, but at the time it was all I could find, and it did have the advantage that I've been relatively safe from Giampaolo here. Mrs Marshall wouldn't have stood for any nonsense from him. However, it won't be easy to find anything now.

I think I'll go and have dinner in a better restaurant than I normally eat in, and I'll have several glasses of wine to neutralise today....

* * *

My imminent eviction was beginning to prey on my mind. Finding accommodation in Lancaster at the moment's about as hard as winning the football pools, and if you start chasing the few rooms advertised around here you're trampled to death in the rush.

Next morning I went to the noticeboard near the central hall of the university where accommodation is advertised. I didn't expect to find anything of any appeal, but for once I was in luck – there was a notice offering two rooms in a reasonable part of Lancaster, not too far from the university. I noted down the contact number, which was a university extension, and raced back to my office and rang it.

'Hullo, Philip Dow here.'

'My name's Christiane Guchez, and I've just seen your advert for two rooms to let.' I was gabbling slightly. 'I'd be very interested to look at them if they haven't gone already.'

'No, I've only just put the notice up, so you're the first to call. When would you like to come round and look at them?'

'Would tomorrow afternoon be all right? I could come today if you'd rather, but tomorrow would suit me better.'

'Tomorrow would be fine by me too. Would about three o'clock be okay, or would you rather earlier or later? I'm guessing that you're working?'

'I am working, but three would be great. I'll see you then.'

Suddenly today seemed a lot brighter – I'd been awake half the night wondering what I'd do if I couldn't find anywhere to live.

The only downside was that the name was Philip Dow. When I was at Cambridge a few years ago I did final year Zoology, and there was a Philip Dow in the same class. The class voted him "most boring of the year", and the thought of living in the same house as him was about as exciting, if it was the same guy. Particularly if the house is tiny. However, I'm desperate so at least I'd better go and see it.

* * *

When I went past the noticeboard later in the day I saw that the advert had disappeared. I hoped that was because of my call, not because someone had beaten me to it.

NEXT DAY

CARLY SMYTH

Heaps of bloody files, that's all I ever see in here. And as fast as I get them processed, more come in. I shouldn't be working here really, because I'm going to become a model. Or an actress. I haven't quite decided which yet.

Anything but Lancaster University, anyway. I wouldn't mind so much if they were nice people to work with, but they're mostly dirty old men in here. Especially my boss.

And just as I was thinking of it, the door opened and he came out. No knocks or anything, no saying may I come through? How would he like it if I burst into his room? I'd probably find him groping that secretary of his, fat Brenda.

'Carlotta, would you take this up to the Vice-Chancellor's office. Immediately, please – it's very urgent.'

I've told him not to call me Carlotta – sounds like a Spanish tart. Don't know what my mother was thinking of when she landed me with that one.

He came round to stand behind me as he dropped it on my desk. He always does that, so he can look down my cleavage. Dirty old sod.

'Yes, Dr Claringbold.'

I didn't make a move straight away, on principle. Why should he boss me around like that? So he stopped in his doorway.

'Immediately, I said', and he glared at me.

'Yes, Dr Claringbold. I'm going straight away.'

I picked up the envelope, which was sealed and had "Staff Confidential" stamped all over it. Probably nude pictures of fat Brenda if I know that lot. I got up, pulled my skirt down as far as it would go, which wasn't very far, and wandered out into the corridor. I wasn't going to overdo it on the speed for that old creep.

As I got to the bottom of the staircase that goes up to the V-C's floor, Phil Dow came out of his office and started heading in the same direction, so I thought I'd play my favourite game with him. I climb up the stairs as slowly as possible, practising my deportment for when I'm a model, and see how slow I have to go before he overtakes me. He probably likes a look as much as any of them, but he's actually not a bad sort. A bit wet, but he's all right.

But it didn't work at all today. He raced past me and up the stairs, and he didn't even seem to notice me.

Must have something on his mind.

PHILIP DOW

This wasn't the best day to have arranged the house viewing. When I fixed the time there was no great problem. Then during the day a couple of disciplinary matters involving staff came up, plus another one of a person who'd accepted a position and hadn't shown up for it. Then the Deputy Vice Chancellor wanted some statistics on staff tenures for a report to the Governing Council. Urgently of course, even though I knew the Council meeting wasn't till next month. That threw out my timetable, but I'm still determined to get to the appointment at home. I've a reason for wanting this one to go right.

I managed to scramble the figures together. Not the best job I've ever done and I hate being sloppy, but I think they were accurate enough for the DVC's needs. I'm never convinced that people read these reports, anyway. No actions ever seem to result from them in my experience.

As I was putting the figures in an envelope the Bursar walked in, and that took another fifteen minutes of discussing whether or not the University should renegotiate its laundry contract. Riveting stuff, to be sure.

I rushed out of my office to take the envelope upstairs, and had to dodge round Carly from the Bursar's office who was doing her usual prance up the stairs. She thinks she's going to become a model or something, so she practises what she calls her deportment around the corridors. It isn't so much deportment as "if you've got it, flaunt it". She certainly has plenty to flaunt, and I've been known to slow down occasionally to enjoy the spectacle, but I reckon the only modelling Carly will get to do will be without clothes on, for men's magazines. Though she might be happy enough with that, anyway.

I managed to get away just after morning tea, and raced home to do some quick cleaning. Today I'm trying to let my upstairs flat, but not just to anyone.

When she rang in response to my advert she gave her name as Christiane Guchez, and there couldn't be two people in the world with a name like that. She must be the person who was in the same final year as me when I was reading Zoology at Cambridge. I didn't know she was even in the university, but apparently she's been working in the computer centre. It has its own administration and they do their own hiring and firing, which is why she hadn't been on my staff list.

Every male in the class wanted to have a relationship with Christiane – including me, of course, though I was nowhere near the front row for that. She actually seemed a nice and natural person, not a siren or anything, but she was one of those females with that indefinable something that attracts any male to her. She probably won't want the flat when she sees it, and if she does she's probably got a string of boyfriends in tow, so it might be rather frustrating anyway, but I'm going to run with it.

I made it home in time and had a quick look round. The place is actually quite clean, but I kept fiddling, moving bits and pieces and then moving them back again. Then in the end I said bugger it – if she doesn't like it the way it is, there's nothing I can do about it. It really mightn't work out all that well anyway.

HERBERT BRIGGS

M r Briggs eyed off the seat with much relief.

Only a few more steps past the loony bin, and then I can sit down on the bench. The stupid doctor's told me to walk here every day, but some days I reckon I'd rather die instead. The only thing that makes it worth it's the chance to watch the passers-by after I've got here. Better than sitting at home with the wife and the telly. Especially if the barmaid with the knockers from the Crown and Feathers comes past. I can't get as far as the Crown and Feathers for a drink any more, and my cow of a wife won't drive me there. I really miss seeing those knockers resting on the counter along with the glasses. Bigger than any of the glasses they were too.

I more or less collapsed on the bench, wedged my stick between the seat slats so I wouldn't lose it, and sat there wheezing. My mate Alfie says I sound like a bloodhound with emphysema, but I can't help it – no lungs much any more. Slowly the puffing eased and I could look at the people who were passing. Like old Mrs Walker, who's on the pavement over the road and going like a crab. Her stick's got four feet on it, and she's walking no better than I do. A year younger than me she is, too. Couple of likely lads – mug you as soon as look at you, like as not. But they didn't pay me any attention, thank God. I don't suppose I look like I'm loaded with money. The postman riding his bike along the footpath – just as well my stick wasn't poking out.

The barmaid with the knockers didn't come past, but one other person did catch my eye. At first I thought it was a good-looking young lad – slim, short fairish hair, walking fast with a fit, springy step. But as the person passed I reckoned it must actually have been a bird. No knockers at all, but moving more like a bird, with a nice swing of the hips and a firm bum. Bit of a fierce expression on her face, though.

A sudden voice came from behind me. 'Top o' the day to ye, Mr Briggs! How's Mrs Briggs this fine afternoon then?'

Bloody hell, watching that bird I hadn't seen the widow O'Meara sneaking up from behind. Until then I could've slumped down and looked as though I was asleep. Too late for that now. I looked again at the young figure striding up the hill, and wished I could still move like that. I'd have given her a run for her money all right.

'Afternoon, Mrs O'Meara. Yes, she's not too bad, thank you kindly, but her rheumatics are playing up again. She's thinking of trying this new diet that was in the paper….'

CHRISTIANE GUCHEZ

I walked up Thwaites Road, past a decrepit old man on a bench who was staring at me, and on past some dismal terrace houses. My face must have been falling by the minute – I'd expected a more appealing area than this one. The houses up the Thwaites Road hill were small terrace houses – two rooms upstairs, two down and a coal hole. A few neat and a lot rather shabby, and no doubt damp as well. Probably houses for mill workers in the earlier days. Inevitable intimacy for anyone living in them, and the thought of sharing them with a male didn't appeal at all. There mightn't be much more space than I have now, and I did have privacy in my present one. Still, I'm desperate so I should at least go and look at the house – then maybe keep on walking.

But there was a surprise at the top of the hill. Thwaites Road turned right and ran along horizontally, just below the crest of the hill. At that level there was a row of quite reasonable and more gracious terrace houses, with three storeys.

And a coal hole, of course.

No. 116 looked in quite good condition. From the size of the windows the rooms would be fairly tall, at least on the ground floor and the first floor. At the top it looked more like an attic. Knowing my luck I'll probably be expected to live in the attic.

I stood on the opposite side of the road and contemplated the house. It certainly had possibilities. There was a small rectangle of concrete in front of the house, softened by two plants in tubs on either side of what was obviously a coal hole cover. There was a solid looking front door, painted in a fresh blue, and beside it was the bay window of a tall front room. With any luck there'd be a window seat inside that – I love window seats.

There seemed no harm in at least looking around the house. No commitment – I could always walk away again. I crossed back over, went up to the front door and rapped the large black doorknocker. A deep sound reverberated through the space behind the door, then footsteps…

PHILIP

I didn't think I was feeling nervous until I heard the door-knocker banging. Then I don't know what I was thinking, but I was sure Christiane wouldn't have remembered me anyway. I've never made much of an impression on people.

I opened the door, and knew instantly that it was the same Christiane. She looked older – not surprisingly since it was seven years since I last saw her – and she looked more strained and weary. But the indefinable something was still there, and it hadn't lost any of its potency.

'Hi, Christiane? Welcome – come on in.'

I couldn't tell whether she recognised me or not. Hopefully not.

She murmured something indistinct which I didn't catch.

Oh well, let's go for it.

'Come in and mind the step, and I'll show you around....'

CHRISTIANE

It was the same Philip. Groan. However, I'd said I was going to look at the house. And I must remember I'm desperate. I need somewhere to live.

I couldn't tell if he remembered who I was, but I suspect he did. I stepped inside.

Because the house was set against a hill there was a step up to the front door, and then just behind the swing of the door there was another step up into a long, thin hallway with a high ceiling. The hall was partly obstructed by a grotesquely ugly creation in wood, rather too big for the passageway, that was hall-stand cum hall table cum hat rack cum umbrella stand cum probably several other things, in a style that was an awful mixture of rococo and Gothic. It had to be Victorian and it was truly hideous.

'I should apologise for this monstrosity, but it's a sort of family heirloom. My father was very keen to get it out of his house, and I thought it might be useful to leave mail and messages on so I said I'd have it. It's probably going to self-destruct soon anyway. It's unbelievably heavy, and every time it's moved it gets more wobbly.'

Not the greatest start.

Past the encumbrance, a door opened on the right into a front room. It was as spacious as I'd guessed from the outside. It had a lounge and two quite comfortable-looking armchairs, the inevitable coffee table, an audio system in gleaming black, a TV, a small sideboard and a tall bookshelf. A selection of books in this last, and a few empty shelves.

And yes! – there was a broad window seat with cushioning all around it. I could almost forgive the hallstand in return for that.

'The tenant can have full use of this room, including the TV and sound system, and you'd be welcome to read any of the books and keep your own on the spare shelves. I'd use the room as well, of course, but I don't actually spend much time in here. I've got a computer upstairs and I use that a lot.'

Next along the corridor a steep staircase led to the upper floors. We passed by that, and the passage continued around a slight bend into the kitchen. At the bend there was a rough door which was closed.

'I won't take you down there unless you want to. It goes into the cellar, but the steps are a bit awkward. The cellar goes under the whole of the house. It's only got a dirt floor, but it's a handy area. Plenty of room for storing empty boxes and suitcases and so on, with wooden pallets to stand things on to keep them clear of any damp. There's a washing machine down there, and clothes lines strung up all round the ceiling for drying washing. The tenant gets to use the machine and all the rest, of course. And there's a workbench and tools as well.'

The kitchen looked quite well set up, though the window that looked on to the backyard was never going to let in much light. You would certainly need lights on inside all the time. The working space wasn't bad, though – a workbench round two of the sides, with a generous-sized sink and a stove inset, plus various wall cupboards. If I had a chance of doing a bit of cooking again I'd love it – I had no access to the kitchen at Mrs Marshall's.

Against the back wall of the kitchen stood a table and two chairs.

'The only thing this house doesn't have is a dining room. I usually eat at this table. You could too if you decide to move in here, or you could eat upstairs in your part which does have a table that you could use as a dining table. But this is the only place to cook, I'm afraid.

'I think the kitchen's got most things a cook needs, and you'd be able to use it all, of course. I reckon we could do it without falling over each other. We'd each be responsible for our own main food, though my suggestion'd be that with basics like sugar, milk, spices and so on, we both use the one supply and whoever notices it's low replaces it.'

I had my doubts about not falling over each other. I value my privacy, and it could be rather a pain.

The end of the kitchen must once have been the back door, but now it opened into a small vestibule with a broom cupboard, coat rack and muddy wellingtons. As we passed the broom cupboard Philip said: 'On the matter of cleaning, I'd ask you to do your two rooms, and I'd clean the rest of the house.'

Two rooms sounded interesting – more than just one attic then. 'That doesn't seem quite fair with the cleaning. The tenant should probably share the general areas, shouldn't they?'

'It doesn't worry me if I do the rest. I'll just be happy not to have to do the rented bit as well. I've been doing it all up to now.'

Fortunately what I'd seen of the house so far looked pretty clean.

From the vestibule a door opened sideways into the backyard, and we went out into it. The yard was small and rather dark.

'The dustbins are at the back – collection's on Wednesdays. There's a clothes line here too, but I don't recommend using it. Neighbours have been losing clothes off their lines, especially women's underwear, which is why I keep the back gate locked except when the dustmen are due. You'd do better to put washing on the lines strung up in the cellar.'

Yuck. Sounds like a charming neighbourhood.

Along a side wall there were a few pots with herbs in them.

'You'd be welcome to use any of the herbs, if you can find any worth picking. The parsley and the thyme are usually okay, but the chives and the oregano struggle. I don't think the oregano likes Lancaster's climate – it's pining for the Mediterranean.'

There was also one tub with rosemary and one with sage, and they looked not too desperate. I do love using fresh herbs in cooking.

At the back of the little vestibule was a bathroom, which had obviously been added later to the house because it looked quite new. It was pleasantly roomy, brightly lit, white with a few blue tiles, and a lavatory, washbasin and bath. All nice and new and clean. The aquamarine bathmat didn't go with the blue tiles, but that could be overlooked. Or fixed.

'This is the main bathroom. I'm hoping to put a shower in some time, but I haven't got round to that yet. There's also a room with toilet and washbasin on the first floor, which is safer at night than trying to get all the way down here. The house is very dark at night.'

Next we climbed the straight and quite steep staircase to the first floor. At the top there were three doors, one to the front and two towards the back of the house. The one at the front opened on to a reasonable sized bedroom, though it was made quite a bit smaller by a double bed and a large wardrobe that took a lot of the space.

'This is my bedroom. The door behind you goes into the small bathroom I was telling you about, and the other room's my study. I was proposing to offer the next floor up to the tenant.'

I knew it – the attic. My heart was sinking still further, even if there were two rooms. God knows what size they'd be.

'That's the staircase to the top floor. Maybe you'd like to go up and have a look and think about it. Then come down and let me know if you're interested. I'll be in the kitchen.'

I thought rather sourly that there probably isn't room for two in the attic. I contemplated bailing out at this stage, but then I remembered my eviction order, and my present bedsitter was very cramped too.

Staircase was not the best name for the access to the top. It was steep – more like climbing a ladder than going up stairs – and it twisted sharply right at the top. Not something you'd be keen to do every day.

But one should never make prior judgements. When I reached the top, the world changed – in fact it became a little world of its own. The staircase opened into two rooms, one front and one back, which were surprisingly roomy. Okay, the ceiling sloped on one side of each because of the roof, but they were hardly cramped and the slope actually gave them character. The front room had a dormer window that looked out over Lancaster, possibly even to Morecambe Bay on a clear day. The bedroom had a large skylight, bathing the room in light, and on tiptoe you could just see what must have been the edge of Lancaster Moor.

The sitting room had an easy chair, a low table, an upright table with chair to serve as a desk or dining table, a standard lamp and a table lamp, and a small bookshelf. The bedroom had a single bed with an attractive bedspread (a simple green vine design), a bedside cabinet with a bedside lamp, a small dressing table, a chest of drawers and a small built-in wardrobe. The central heating from the rest of the house even extended up to this level, and both rooms were beautifully neat and clean.

I would have far more room than I'd had at Mrs Marshall's, and I'd be able to use the kitchen to cook for myself which would be a real plus. My mother had had a number of goes at teaching me to cook properly, and I also hung around her feet a lot when she was in the kitchen, so a few further skills went in by osmosis and cooking became a real pleasure.

And better than all of that, climbing up to these rooms was like entering a sanctuary above the real world. I need a place where my ex won't find me, and this might just be it.

I kicked my shoes off and lay down on the bed to think. The rooms were very tranquil. The front room was very pale grey and easy on the eye. The bedroom was the same shade of grey but with the faint design of a plant vine on the wallpaper, echoing the bedspread, and it was even more restful to look at.

The bed was comfortable too, and I was almost dozing when a seagull landed on the roof, gripping at the frame of the bedroom skylight with a rattle of its claws against the glass. It peered in through the window and seemed to be looking directly at me. Ugly as the bird was, it was almost like a welcome.

It suddenly occurred to me that other people might be coming to look at the rooms and I could miss out. I jumped off the bed and went down to the kitchen.

Philip was weighing flour on kitchen scales.

'The upper rooms are very nice. I'd certainly be interested if they're still available.'

'No problem – you're the first person to look at them. You phoned me twenty minutes after I put the notice up, so I took it down again. I know how much pressure there is on rooms in Lancaster at the moment and there was no way I was going to be bombarded with pestering phone calls. My plan was to take the notice down every time someone showed interest, and put it back up if they didn't want the rooms. I knew they'd be taken by someone soon enough. So if you want them, they're yours. Why don't we have a cup of coffee and discuss the details?'

He had a small espresso machine, and when the coffee came it was good. He pushed the scales and the flour to the back of the bench.

'I was about to make some biscuits, but that can wait. So when would you like to move in?'

I hesitated. 'I'm supposed to give four weeks' notice at my present place. I'm paid up till the end of next week, but my landlady wants the room as soon as possible for her daughter who's pregnant and hasn't got anywhere to live. I'm sure she won't mind if I leave sooner.'

'If there's no reason against it, why not straight away? I've taken the rest of the day off work because I didn't know how long this was going to take, and I've got my car. I could help you shift stuff over. I wouldn't start the rent until the end of next week, when your credit with your landlady's passed.'

'That doesn't seem fair if I'm in the rooms. I couldn't do that.'

'In the normal run of things I might possibly agree, but there's actually a reason for it. I bought this house with some money left to the family by my Great Great Aunt Clarissa, whose hallstand you've already encountered. Now you know why I keep the hallstand. Her will said that if possible the money should be used "to further the equality between the sexes". I'm a male living here, so for equality it has to be a female, and I'm sure Aunt Clarissa wouldn't have wanted you to pay double rent for her house.'

'And what if you'd had a man applying to rent the place?'

He looked a bit embarrassed. 'If a guy had rung I'd have said the rooms were already taken. If a female phoned I was going to invite her to look at the place. It was the only way I could think of to do it. If I'd put "only women need apply" you can imagine how many calls I'd have got – or not. Or what sort of callers they'd have been if there were any.'

It sounded plausible though rather unlikely, but the upstairs rooms were nice and I was desperate. I'm fairly resilient, and I can probably cope if problems arise.

'It's very kind of you. Thank you, and thanks to Aunt Clarissa as well. She sounds quite a lady.'

'I believe she was. She was a very active suffragette, and she lived to quite an age. She died before I was born, but my mother met her once or twice. Mum used to say she was like a fierce dragon but with a lovely twinkle in her eye. I'd love to have known her, though I'd probably have been terrified of her. Anyway, back to the present. D'you have much stuff to shift?'

'Not a huge amount, and half of it's still packed because my room was so small I couldn't get it in.'

'In that case, why don't I quickly show you the cellar and you can decide what stuff you want to put down there in storage and what's to go upstairs. Then I can drop you over, and I'll pick up the full boxes and bring them back here while you pack the rest. I'll come back afterwards to collect you and the remainder.'

'That'd be terrific, thank you. I don't think I deserve this treatment.'

He didn't say anything, so he probably agreed.

The cellar steps were just a sort of broad ladder, leading into a large area that obviously ran under most of the house. I saw the laundry space, with the washing lines strung all around, and the workbench and various storage cupboards. It was surprisingly clean and neat. At the front, where the coal probably used to be delivered, there was wooden boarding laid down and a few cases and boxes were heaped up there.

'Anything you want to store can go there. It's quite dry.'

We went back upstairs, and he said: 'You won't be in a position to cook for yourself tonight, so on Aunt Clarissa's behalf I'll do a simple meal for both of us. After that I'll leave you in peace – I promise.'

I keep getting a feeling that I'm being engineered into something, and God knows what the cooking will be like, but I couldn't think of any valid objections so we did the shift.

* * *

In the end it was all fine. Mrs Marshall was out when I collected my stuff, so I just left her the keys and a note on the kitchen table to tell her what I'd done. She'd complain no end to the neighbours about how she'd been cheated, but she was getting a free week's rent and I knew she'd be happy to have the room for her daughter straight away.

I began to unpack and get myself organised. I did actually have a lot more room here than in Mrs Marshall's. Soon after I'd started Philip called up my stairway: 'Would dinner at about seven fifteen tonight suit you?'

'Fine by me. Thank you very much – I wouldn't really be organised to cook food at the moment.'

'I just thought I'd do a simple risotto tonight.'

My heart sank then. I'd been married to an Italian who cooked as good a risotto as anyone in his home country. Most people in Britain who cook think a risotto's just an ordinary savoury rice. At least I won't be having to cook tonight, though.

I went down soon after seven. The kitchen was bright and cheerful and there was a pleasant smell of cooking. Philip waved at a bottle of wine on the table.

'Pour yourself a glass if you like – I'm already under way.'

I was expecting something like a Chianti, but it was actually an Australian cabernet.

'I'm aiming to have this ready at quarter past. I'm sure you'll know that a risotto shouldn't wait once it's ready, and I didn't know how organised you'd be with your unpacking.'

The wine was nice, and the risotto when it came was even better, against all my expectations. It had sautéed veal with fresh sage, some interesting mushrooms, fresh corn kernels and green beans, and it was cooked to perfection.

As we ate, I said: 'When you said risotto I was a bit worried because I was married at one stage to a top risotto maker. Giampaolo could have won competitions if he tried. And most of the British don't even have any idea of what a real risotto is.'

'Yes, well, I was in that category for quite a while too. My moment of revelation came when someone told me what types of rice you have to use to make proper risotto. When I was a student I used to make risotto using ordinary long grain rice and it never came out like the ones in good Italian restaurants. Then I was told about arborio and I haven't looked back. Though this is actually carnaroli – it's the last of some I picked up at an Italian shop in London some weeks ago. The third one I was told about is vialone nano, but I haven't been able to find anyone who stocks that yet. I hope to try it one day. But for the moment I'll stick with carnaroli if I can keep getting it – I think it makes an even better risotto than arborio.'

I wasn't going to admit it, but I couldn't remember exactly which sort of rice Paolo used, though it must have been one of those.

We toasted Great Great Aunt Clarissa with the cabernet.

The risotto was followed by fresh raspberries with a little ice cream – "to clear the palate" – and then we drank some green tea.

I lay in bed that night and looked through the skylight at stars in the night sky. Today had seemed more like a dream than my usual reality. I just hoped I wasn't going to wake up again any time soon.

FRANK ELLIOTT

When I'm feeling mischievous I like to tell people I've spent the last twenty years in a mental hospital. The variety of looks that go across their faces is right funny, and nobody knows what to say. Then I add that it's as a pest control officer, and this huge sense of relief goes across them. And then you add the final comment that the standard joke around the hospital is that you can't tell the staff from the patients.

In some cases there's a bit of truth in that, too. I always remember one night when I had to work late, I turned a corner into one of the long corridors and I saw in the distance one of the doctors who looks after the sanity of the patients. He stood out with his white coat, and he was up against one of the doors. The doors are real tall, and they have brass doorknobs that are about the size and shape of a well-formed titty. The doc was fondling one of the doorknobs, and he was having such a good time doing it that he never even saw me. Thank God.

Me dad thought me whole job were a good joke, and he used to tell all his friends about his son who was in the 'bin', but me mam couldn't abide by it. She used to tell her friends that

I worked for the National Health Service. Which were true, of course. I think the National Health Service is the biggest employer in Lancaster since the cotton mills closed their doors.

It isn't a bad job on the whole. At least I'm not in the big psychiatric hospital up the road. That's got a lot of locked wards, and me mate up there has to be quite careful when he goes into some parts. I'm in the Royal Victoria Hospital, which was set up for those patients who are called 'simple'. I was reading the little sheet that the hospital gives to all staff wi' the history of it, and it said that the hospital were founded in 1868 as "a small asylum for idiots", and that's just about right. We've got a few tricky ones, of course, but for the most part they're harmless and even quite good fun. Some of 'em could probably live back in the general community if they had the chance, but their families probably didn't want 'em, or there's no family left any more.

We've got a number of locked wards too, but that's for the sake of the patients not the outside community. The patients have no idea who they are or where they are, and they'd just wander off and get run over when they got to the main road. We only have the one which is locked for the safety of everybody. It's up inside the tower which is the centre of the hospital building. Luckily for me they don't get many pest problems there.

I get a free run round the whole of the hospital, except for one room way up in the central tower above the locked ward. It's firmly closed off and I don't even know who has the key. From what I've heard it's a bit of a black museum, wi' some of the bits and pieces they used to use in the olden days – strait-jackets, leg irons and the like. I guess they wouldn't like the public to hear about that now. Meself, I wouldn't mind havin' a look at it just the once, to know.

Some of the patients get fits every now and then. There's a fair number that wear fit caps – padded things covering the whole top and sides of the head, so if they get a fit and fall they don't hurt themselves too much. I think with some of them it's because they bang their heads against the walls deliberately, too. Others wear padded jackets, for the same sort of reason I suppose, and others again have their hands covered in things like big padded gloves.

It took me a bit of time to get used to some of the more extreme wards. People with very low mental ages – for some reason they can't abide having clothes on. If the nurse dresses 'em they strip off as soon as they can, and some of 'em try to flush their clothes down the toilet which of course blocks the drains. The sewer man, Tommy, isn't too impressed wi' that. I don't mind it so much – Tommy has to use his big lifter to get the cover off, and then I get a chance to spray some of the cockroaches that are always there in the drains.

The other thing I couldn't get used to at first was that those same patients would sit in their chairs, rocking back and forth and mekkin' a sort of keening sound. It reminds me of some of our relatives when they go to a funeral, and I always find it a bit unnerving.

In wards like that the smell's pretty horrible. Piss and shit and puke all mixed up together, combined with the sickly sweet disinfectant that the staff use to try and clean it all up. You get used to it after a while, but it still wrinkles me nose up when I first go into a ward like that. In some of those wards the patients smear shit over their faces and bodies, too.

There's one ward in the hospital that I've never got used to, though. It's called the Infirmary. I think it gets the occasional patients who need hospital-type treatment, but it mostly houses youngish kids with terribly distorted limbs. They have to lie on things like giant bean bags because their limbs stick out every which way, and their twisted shapes wouldn't fit into any chairs. So they lie there all day, unable to do anything really, and they let out these awful moans and screams. They say that a person who hears the screams of someone being burnt to death hears those screams for the rest of their lives. I think I'll be hearing these ones forever too. The really terrifying thing is that I'm not sure that all of those kids are 'simple', as they call it. And if they're in that predicament and they can fully understand their condition and their prospects, to my mind that'd be the total vision of hell on earth. I just hope I'm wrong.

Makes you thankful to be reasonably normal yourself, though I always think of the old Yorkshire saying: "All t'world's mad but thee and me, and thee's a bit queer."

CHRISTIANE

It looks like the house-sharing arrangement's working out okay, at least from my point of view. Philip isn't as gruesome as I'd feared he was going to be. He just seems to be a bit socially disconnected, and I can't quite work out why. I don't see all that much of him which is fine by me. I prefer a fair bit of privacy, which I do get here. Philip spends a lot of time in his study, presumably at his computer. God knows what he does there all the time. He doesn't seem to have much of a social life – not much of any sort of life that's obvious.

I guess I haven't got much of a life at the moment either, but I'm not yet ready to get out again. Not when Paolo may still be out there. I'm keeping a low profile, tucked in my office at work and in this house the rest of the time. But I almost have the run of the house, and life's comfortable if quiet.

Every now and then Philip and I bump into each other, but he isn't a nuisance. We don't clash over the bathrooms much, and we usually meet in the kitchen if anywhere. Occasionally we share a brew of coffee if one of us has one on the go.

On one such morning I'd made coffee and Philip dug out some shortbread biscuits that he'd just baked. I'm quite fond of shortbread, and these were surprisingly good.

We sat for a bit longer than usual, and I asked him:

'How come you're in administration when you're a zoologist?'

'Couldn't get a job. I came up north intending to work for the Nature Conservancy at Grange-over-Sands. I'd had a half-promise of a position, but it fell through at the last minute – they said they had absolutely no funds. So then I tried the Freshwater Biological Association at Windermere. Nothing going there either – they sounded even more broke than the Nature Conservancy. My final hope was to get some sort of scientific position in the university here, but there didn't seem to be anything relevant to my background. It was all rather depressing. My present admin job's all I could get in the end. I'm the second in charge of general staffing at the uni. It's not exactly thrilling, but it's okay. It's a salary, and it does have a few interesting moments. But don't ask me to describe them because they're pretty few and far between. How about you – same problem?'

'I did get a job at first, at Cambridge as a research assistant. It was with Professor Ramsay estimating snail populations at Wicken Fen. Then I had to move away from Cambridge rather suddenly for personal reasons, and I haven't been able to get a job in Zoology since. But the snail project involved a lot of computer analysis, and I've been able to squeeze myself into computer-related work ever since.'

Then we started talking about our social lives at university – I can't quite remember how it came up.

Philip said: 'I didn't get much of a look-in with English

girls. They were all too busy chasing exotic, aristocratic or well-heeled guys. I was regarded as totally dull – in fact I heard I won the class vote as the least exciting male of the year. I guess I could understand why, but it wasn't very kind. Luckily there were one or two around who were a bit more forgiving.'

I raised my eyebrows but didn't say anything.

'For more than a year I had a Malaysian Chinese girlfriend, who taught me all sorts of new things.'

'Sex' I murmured, then could have bitten my tongue. I hadn't meant to say it aloud.

Philip gave me a somewhat startled look. 'Well, not in the sense of losing my virginity, if that's what you mean. That happened when I was fifteen. Our sixteen year old neighbour got hold of a sex manual and wanted someone to practise with. Though at chapter two she discovered that older men were more interesting and she dropped me.

'Lucy took me forward a chapter or two, but that wasn't what I meant. She just had an interest in so many different things in life. She'd travelled, she knew about different cultures, she taught me about Chinese food and even a bit how to cook it. When we parted we'd been planning a trip to northern Thailand, to one of the hill tribe areas. I was quite excited about that. And a bit apprehensive because I've never been further than France before, but I thought with somebody Asian alongside me I'd be okay. We'd even started trying to learn one of the hill tribe languages, though that was definitely a challenge.'

'Why did you part? It sounds as though it was quite a rewarding relationship.'

'Lucy was an odd person. She had a good head for money and business, and she was totally mercenary. She always said she came to Britain to find a rich husband, and she slept around ruthlessly in pursuit of one. I didn't fit any of her categories, but I think I was her relaxation from the chase after a fortune because she knew I had no prospects at all. At least not anything that she'd be interested in. We just enjoyed life together.

'I knew it wouldn't last – she made that quite clear. But I was enjoying it while it did last, and I could overlook her liaisons with the other men. We had a tacit arrangement that she met the others in their rooms, and her apartment was for us.

'However, one day I went round to her place to drop off a travel guide to Thailand. I had my own keys and I let myself in, and then I heard sounds from the bedroom. I went quietly up the hallway. The door was open and I could see the large mirror that she had over the bed. She always enjoyed the visual element of sex. The mirror showed her lowering herself on to the upstanding member of the sitting member for Lancaster East. She always did like to be on top, in everything.

'It was a shock to find that happening in what I'd thought of as "our" area, and I felt betrayed. They hadn't noticed me – they were far too occupied. On the spur of the moment I left the guidebook in the middle of the kitchen table with my keys on it, and I let myself out. She would have understood when she saw it. She never tried to contact me again. I later regretted the sudden impulse, though it was probably for the best in the end. It was always going to finish some time.'

It was a curious little story, but I wasn't going to get involved on personal subjects with Philip. I said 'Lucy's an odd name for a Chinese Malaysian.'

'She acquired it when she came to Cambridge, before I met her. Two parts of her name were Lee and Soo, so her classmates switched it to Lucy. I think she quite liked the Anglicisation.'

'You must have been a bit disappointed about Thailand. That would have been quite exciting.'

'Yes, but it was also going to be challenging. D'you have any idea of some of the things they eat in places like that? At least in the hill tribe areas. The section on food in the guidebook said they eat things like raw meat marinated in bile, and cooked cow's placenta. I don't mind trying new and different foods – quite enjoy it, in fact, but probably not to that extent.'

'Did you get to learn any of the language in the end?'

He snorted. 'Hardly. It was fiendish. We were thinking of going to a Lisu area, northwest of Chiang Mai towards the border with Myanmar. Let me get my crib sheet where I started to put down phrases.'

He went upstairs and came back with a piece of paper.

'Look at this one. To say "Do you have any water – I'd like a little to drink" you have to say "water have not have, I one bit drink", and in Lisu it looks like this.' He held out the sheet which read: "Aljjai jjuaq mat jjuaq, ngua tit ket ddox". 'Don't even think of asking me how you pronounce it – I never came to grips with it. I think even Lucy would have been challenged on that stuff.'

The coffee had gone by then and we drifted out of the kitchen. I wondered afterwards why Philip didn't seem to have a girlfriend now. I'd been thinking that maybe he was gay, but apparently not. The tale of Lucy suggested otherwise, though in my experience the thing that men lie about more than anything is their sex life and their sexual conquests.

Maybe Philip's just asexual now. He certainly hasn't tried to make any sort of pass at me. Thank God.

What was striking me about Philip though, living in the same house as him, was that he wasn't so much boring as lacking in some sort of ability to interact socially with people. He wasn't in fact boring – that was a misjudgement by the zoology class – but you couldn't help feeling that something just wasn't there. There was a feeling of something zombie-like, but I had no idea what might underlie something like that. And I couldn't say whether it bothers him or not – that's another thing he doesn't give away.

PHILIP

Today was slightly curious. I had to interview an applicant for a position to manage the university catering services, and I'd picked someone called Rosemary Mason from a rather small pile of applications. She was well qualified, and I hoped that she'd have the right personality for managing a rather diverse team of staff.

She turned up punctually – always a good start, because not all interviewees do. She was neatly presented, and looked a pleasant person – a little nervous as she came in, but then so are many interviewees. Me too when I came for this job, actually – I needed something rather desperately at the time.

'Good morning, Rosemary Mason is it? I'm Philip Dow, the second in charge of recruitment for the university.'

'I'm Rosemary, yes. It's good of you to take the time to see me.'

'Well, your resumé was very relevant.' Put them at their ease – makes it easier to get them to speak freely. 'I noticed that you started with Campbell and Fortescue in Preston – would you like to tell me how you found that job?'

'Well, it was advertised in the paper.'

'No, I meant what did you find them like to work for, and what was the job like?' I grinned to try and suggest to her it was my misunderstanding.

'It was a very pleasant place to work in. The management was always considerate to the employees. I started just organising the storeroom. They're an old-fashioned family grocer, and they had hundreds of different things in their storeroom. It took a fair bit of organisation to sort them all out and know where they were at a moment's notice. Anyway, they must have liked what I was doing, because after a bit they put me in charge of a couple of the other staff.'

'How did that go down with the others? Had they been there longer than you?'

'Yes, they had, but they didn't want to take too much responsibility so they were quite happy if I organised them a bit. I tried to treat them with consideration, like the shop did with me.'

What she was saying was encouraging, and the way that she said it was also good – calm and confident, but with no sense of boasting.

Then we ran through the next steps in her career. Up to a certain point she gave a clear and confident account of each position. Then, when we got to a period in her life and career about five years ago she suddenly became vague, and more than that she seemed a bit agitated. That isn't totally unusual in my experience – it can be a marital breakup or something, and people don't want to be reminded of it or simply don't want to talk about it. Nothing wrong there, but Rosemary Mason's reaction was certainly stronger than any I'd ever seen before.

Then with more recent work she was all right again, and the interview concluded very positively.

After she'd gone I thought hard about what she'd said – and what she hadn't. She wasn't obviously different from many people who I've interviewed who've been a bit tentative about bits of their career, but a little niggle of instinct told me that there was a bit more to it in her case.

However, when I weighed it all up I decided that she seemed normal, well-balanced and competent now, and totally well suited for the quite complex task of catering manager. It isn't really my position to judge her on past things unless they might affect her job with us, and I didn't think that any of that was very likely to. I got a reference from her most recent employer, and it said that she was a steady, calm and effective worker. They seemed to be genuine about it, rather than someone wanting to get rid of a worker from their workplace. I had no hesitation in drafting a recommendation that she be offered the position, and I was hoping that the university administration would agree.

AGGIE RANSOME

I was happy at home till Uncle Bertie came. There was just me, Mum and Dad. Dad was at work a lot, but me and Mum got on well and we both laughed a lot.

Then when I was thirteen Uncle Bertie came to stay. He was Mum's brother. I thought at first he'd just come for a visit, but he never showed any signs of leaving again.

He seemed quite friendly, but I never felt quite at ease when he was around. And it was never quite as easy with Mum after he came.

Uncle Bertie kept telling me how pretty I was, and after a while I wished he wouldn't. It was a bit creepy. When Dad was working and Mum had gone out shopping or something, he sometimes put his arm around me and told me I was pretty, and he even kissed me. I told him I wasn't happy with that, but he said that a man must tell a girl how nice she is. I thought about telling Mum, but I was embarrassed, and he was her brother so she mightn't be happy with me.

I noticed that he never put his arm around me when Mum

was there, so I thought he knew it wasn't right himself.

Then Uncle Bertie started patting me on the bum. I told him to stop it, but he wouldn't. And then he put his hand in my knickers and started to rub me. I shouted out that he mustn't, but he said it was because I was so pretty that he couldn't help it.

He said: "D'you notice the bulge in the front of my trousers? That's what happens when a man sees a beautiful girl." And he opened his trousers and showed me, and made me stroke and pat the awful thing. I was horrified and really frightened. I wanted to run away, but the door was firmly shut.

And one day he pulled my knickers off violently and pushed his thing into me. The pain was terrible and I screamed and begged him not to, but he told me that it was my fault for being so pretty and he couldn't help himself.

Then one day Mum came home early as he had his thing out and was making me rub it. She went completely white, and then screamed loudly. Uncle Bertie quickly closed up his trousers and said he was sorry, but it was my fault because I'd been undressing in front of him and asking him to do things.

I cried and said I'd never done that, but Mum didn't want to listen to me and I was sent to my room in disgrace.

But even worse, later on I felt some changes inside me and it turned out that a baby was growing in me. I was sent away to a hospital so that the baby could be taken away. I'd thought that after that I could go home again, but instead I was sent to another hospital.

This hospital.

The loony bin.

Apparently I was "morally defective", and not fit to be among normal people.

As far as I know Uncle Bertie remained at home, but they never contacted me again so I never really knew.

PHILIP

One evening Christiane happened to mention that she plays squash. I'm a reasonable player myself and I haven't found anyone to play with recently, so I asked her if she'd like a game sometime and she agreed. We fixed it for the coming Saturday morning, and I was quite looking forward to it.

* * *

On the day she looked trim and athletic in her white squash gear.

The pleasurable expectation of the squash lasted about a minute into the warm-up – maybe less. I may have been a reasonable squash player but Christiane was somewhere around national class. Or Olympic or something like that. I was completely outclassed.

I hoped that she might just have been faster than I was to warm up but when we started to play I found my sinking feeling was fully justified. I was manoeuvred all over the place; the ball whistled regularly past me and exactly into the back corner, or past my front to die against the side wall. I tried my hardest but I hardly got more than a point a game, and I got crosser and crosser at my inability to make any impression.

Finally I said in complete frustration: 'You might have warned me you played at this level. I wouldn't have wasted your time then.'

She gave me an angry look. 'I wouldn't have thought you'd be a bad loser. Surely you knew that I got a blue at Cambridge for squash?'

'Well, I didn't know and I wouldn't have subjected either of us to this if I had.'

'If that's how you feel, forget it. I'll find my way home.' Tight-lipped, she disappeared.

* * *

I stood in the court, now a solitary figure, and in frustration whacked a number of balls as hard as I could at the front wall. However, it didn't help so I went home.

I was so angry for a while that I didn't care, but in time I realised it was stupid, especially on my part. I don't think it was that I was a bad loser – more that I felt I was completely wasting Christiane's time, and I was embarrassed at having done so. I'd also looked like a complete idiot, but at least I'm more used to that.

It wouldn't have been so bad if I'd had some warning. I don't know that I could have known that she was a blue, though she'd obviously expected it. There were plenty of sportspeople around Cambridge who represented the university, and unless you were directly involved with them you wouldn't really know.

Anyway, I figured it was up to me to make amends, so when we overlapped in the kitchen a couple of days later I said: 'About the squash the other day, I'm sorry for my temper and carry-on. I just felt completely frustrated that I couldn't have given you a better game. Or any sort of game, in fact. I just felt that I was wasting your time completely.'

She gave me a hard look. 'Okay, I've been waiting for you to apologise to tell you that you actually gave me the best contest I've had since I've been in Lancaster. You're not a bad player. If you could ever swallow your pride enough to have another game with me I could show you how to get several more points in a game off me.' She picked up her coffee and wandered off, but a sort of truce had been declared.

Relations remained cool for a while, but at least we were talking again.

FRANK ELLIOTT

Being a pest controller in an old Victorian hospital like this one's a challenge in some ways – not least because the building has walls that are about six foot thick or more. And over time things have moved a bit, so there's plenty of cracks and deep spaces where pests can hide away.

Of all the pests that plague the hospital, the meanest is the Pharaoh's ant. It's so tiny that it can hide away in the smallest spaces, and there's hundreds of those. Spaces, that is – there's bloody millions of the ants. They're all through the cracks in the ancient walls, and you just can't get at 'em with any chemicals – they won't penetrate deep enough. And the ants' cruellest activity is that they get into the wards and invade the patients' lockers, where they get into anything that's edible.

Most of the patients haven't got any family – at least nobody who bothers to acknowledge 'em – and the one special thing that happens to 'em is that the nurses buy or bake a birthday cake just for them on their one day of the year. And then I get the call about a Pharaoh's ant outbreak, and I find the cake invisible under an extra icing of thousands of tiny orange bodies, swarming all over it. All you can do then is throw the cake away and try to stem the tears and cheer the patient up again.

Because us humans can't get any chemical treatment into the massive walls, me counterpart at the Moor Hospital's trying to develop a bait loaded with poison that the ants'll take back inside the walls themselves. It mustn't act too quickly or it'll kill the ants before it gets taken back into the nest, but it's got to be poisonous enough that it does kill 'em all in the end. It's a fine balancing act, and I'm not sure that me mate's version's working all that well yet. He gave me a sample once, but it didn't seem to kill many of me Pharaohs.

The other pests that I really don't like are rats. They're very smart and they're secretive. I've also heard that they can spread some nasty diseases, though thank God we don't seem to have had any of the diseases in the hospital.

Trying to do anything against the rats also has some extra challenges here compared to what a normal pest controller would face. When you put rat bait down you have to find somewhere where the rats'll come and feed on it, but it's also got to be somewhere where the patients won't find the bait and eat it. They think the made-up bait pellets look like sweeties. You also don't want to spray over things like fag ends that've been thrown away. They absorb the spray, and the patients quite often pick 'em up and suck 'em. I usually try to bait with a mixture that I make up meself – pinhead oatmeal with the poison for rats, and canary seed with poison for mice.

I rarely find any dead rats or mice – mebbe they crawl away somewhere to die. The only rat I definitely know I killed were one that stuck its head out of a drain at the wrong moment, when I were holding an iron bar. One wallop and it were history.

The pests that are favourites wi' the patients are the cockroaches. They call 'em blackclocks in these parts, and they love to come round wi' me when I'm looking for infestations. Which are often in the drains, and the patients love that too. They offer to climb into the drains to get the blackclocks out for me, and I have to nip that in the bud. Also, some of the patients reckon that I kill the blackclocks by biting 'em in half, and I have to stop 'em trying that too. They mek do wi' stamping on 'em instead. The blackclocks mek a sharp cracking noise that the patients just love.

I guess I'm lucky – I really only have rats and mice and cockroaches and ants to deal with. Some places'd get a lot more pests than that. I do get the occasional bird that comes into a ward, most often sparrers, but that's only a matter of catching 'em and evicting 'em, and they're usually as keen as I am to get 'em out again. And I did once get a swarm of bees that settled in one of the wards, but that only needed a phone call to the local beekeepers who sent someone round to collect the swarm. I enjoyed that, actually, watching how the beekeeper persuaded the swarm to go into his collection box, like a little hive.

And my other luck is that I only have to deal with pests off the patients – ones on the body like crabs are nursing problems, not mine. Thank God. I used to be surprised that in a home like this they'd get crabs, and I asked one of the charge nurses once. He looked at me like I were a bit simple meself, and said: "Same way as you or I'd get 'em – havin' a bit o' nookie wi' someone who's got 'em already." I said I didn't think that'd happen in a place like this, and he just said: "They may be daft, but they're not that daft!"

My other fun occupation is helping the drains guy, Tommy, to clear blocked drains – usually when the patients strip their gear off and flush the clothes down the toilet. It's not so bad if they rip them into shreds first – then they keep going down the sewers, but if they're whole they either get stuck in the bowl or they go a certain distance and then get stuck on a bend. It can take the two of us a while to get 'em out again if they're in an awkward spot. We've got a couple of poles with metal hooks on the end, and you can usually snag the clothes with 'em after a while. All good fun.

I actually don't mind working here. It's like a sort of community, and most of the patients are quite gentle – just a bit simple. I got my original training at the Moor Hospital, and I got quite spooked by some of the violent patients there. Me mate up there says you get used to it after a while, and you learn how to watch out for yourself, but I'm not so sure. He's welcome to it.

It's not quite as easy here though for some of the nursing staff, specially them in the more extreme wards. Often when I'm poking around behind filing cabinets and cupboards and the like I'll find a half empty bottle of whisky. I guess they've got to have something to take the pressure off.

I do get away some of the time – I've got a couple of night jobs, the main one being pest control up at the university computer centre. I thought it'd be good getting away from the weird atmosphere of the nuthouse, but you'd have to say that a few of the people up there at the uni are about as strange as some of our patients. My main contact's there's a really nice lass, though – Christina. She makes the whole thing worthwhile.

And the money, of course.

PHILIP

The catering manager position's becoming a bit of a problem. The university administration duly agreed to the appointment of Rosemary Mason, as I'd expected, and I mailed her a letter of offer. Almost a week later there'd been no reply, so I phoned the number that she'd given me. It rang and rang, but there was no reply.

I called again the next day with the same result. By that stage it was getting a bit more urgent to get a catering manager, so I went round to the address given on her application. The house was a typical suburban one, undistinguished in any way. It looked completely closed up and had all the curtains drawn. Several bottles of milk stood near the front door, and there was a general feel that the place had been quiet for a while.

I left it for another day, and then I went round again. Same result – and the milk bottles were still there and the curtains hadn't moved an inch from where they were the day before. I thought back then to her odd reaction in part of the interview, and wondered if for some reason she'd done a sudden bunk. Maybe something from the past that she hadn't revealed had caught up with her, or maybe she needed to hide something and couldn't face taking on the job. But that seemed odd given that she'd been working steadily and well in a similar job in Lancaster. Why would the university suddenly threaten everything?

One of the neighbours came out of her house at that stage, so I asked if she knew where Rosemary was. She didn't know a thing, and she hardly seemed to know Rosemary's name.

This was all getting stranger and stranger. I gave it one more day and then went back to the house, where still nothing had changed. At that point I had to consult with the administration, and we agreed that we couldn't keep on with Rosemary – we had to look for an alternative. My heart sank then because I'd been uncharacteristically lazy with this interview process – I should always do at least two applicants. But in this case Rosemary was so clearly the best, ahead of an otherwise rather dismal bunch, so I'd interviewed only her. Now I had to call in the next best candidate for an interview which meant further delay. It served me right for being lazy, but I was so sure Rosemary would be the one.

And it was sad because the next one down the line really wasn't anywhere close to Rosemary in her experience and abilities.

LANCASTER POLICE HQ

Inspector Brady was becoming irritated. He threw the file on to his desk with a loud slap. Several papers fell out and were retrieved by Sergeant Nielsen.

'How the hell can we still have this bloody female unidentified, eh? How the hell can nobody have missed her in five weeks? Nearly six. It's ridiculous, we've checked every bloody missing report – not a tally. It's almost as though she wasn't a real person. But she's a real body, and she was strangled by a real person. This isn't going to look good in the reports.'

'We're still checking up on one new report of a missing woman in Huddersfield, sir.'

'Oh, bollocks to Huddersfield! That lead'll be as dead as all the rest. They're all as dead as the woman herself.'

At which point he picked up the phone that was buzzing on his desk.

'Local man, you say? Okay, send him up.'

He looked at Sergeant Nielsen.

'You won't believe this. A Lancaster man has just called in

to report a woman who's been missing for a couple of weeks. Jesus wept! If it's our one, why couldn't he have come forward before now?'

A young man, of fairly slender build and a bit above medium height, was shown into the office.

'Good morning. My name's Philip Dow. I called in to report a woman who seems to have gone missing, and I was worried in case something might have happened to her. They asked me to come and see Inspector Brady.'

He looked at them expectantly.

'I'm Brady. This is Sergeant Nielsen. Now, sir, would you like to tell us what this is all about?'

'I'm the second in charge of general staffing at the university. Some weeks ago we advertised for someone to manage the university catering services. We got a number of applicants, and the best by a wide margin was a woman called Rosemary Mason. At least that was what she said her name was.'

Brady looked at Nielsen at that comment, but didn't say anything.

'We asked her to come in for an interview, and we asked her to bring her birth certificate and social security documents so we could note them to save time later. She did this, and we noted down that her birth certificate showed her to be Rosemary Mason – no other names. Then we wrote to her offering the job, but we never had a reply.

'After a week I phoned, but there was no reply. I phoned again – still nothing. I went round to the house, in Merrington Road – nobody home. I went round a couple of times because I'd got a bit curious by that stage, but it was always the same. Nobody home, all the windows closed and the curtains drawn, but you can just see that there's still furniture inside the house so it didn't look as though she'd done a flit.

'I asked the neighbours, but they said they hardly ever saw her anyway, so they hadn't noticed any difference. But they reckoned they'd have noticed if there'd been furniture vans or anything. So then we had to give the job to somebody else – we couldn't wait.'

'Well, sir, your case isn't all that unusual, I have to tell you. People disappear quite regularly. Some part of their past catches up with them. Or they're getting away from a lover. With a woman it might be a separated spouse who hasn't accepted that they're separated – you'd be surprised how often that happens. However, you seemed to have some doubt about the lady's real name. Would you like to tell me about it?'

Philip coloured a little.

'Well, I suppose I shouldn't have done it really, but I don't think it was illegal. I have a sideline of chasing up people's family histories for them – I did it once for my family and I got to know my way around the records, so I thought I could make a few bob extra doing it for other people.

'I just happened to have the microfiches out the other day, and I thought I'd check the entry for the lady I couldn't find in the flesh. I don't know why I did it really, because her birth certificate seemed absolutely genuine, but the funny thing is that she wasn't there. I checked very carefully, several times, and there's no record of her birth as given on her certificate. There may be nothing in it, but I just thought I'd better tell someone official in case there's something phoney, and then you can do what you like with it.'

He made as though to get up.

'Hang on a minute, sir. There may be some innocent explanation, but it is a little unusual if you're right. Can you give us a description of the lady, sir?'

'Well, it's been a little while since I saw her, but I do study people quite carefully as part of the interview process. She was about five foot two in height, maybe a bit less, dark hair, medium length and pinned up fairly severely. She had a slightly husky voice, I remember, and a faint tic in the left eye. I had a slight feeling that she might have once had an injury to the side of the face that was associated with it, but if so it was only a hint. The thing that I did notice, though, when she handed over her documents, was that her right hand had several scars across the back as though she'd been injured in an accident, and one of the finger joints was a little distorted.'

'Bloody hell, it's her!' said Brady to Nielsen. 'We've found her at last.'

He turned to Philip.

'Sir, I'm going to have to ask you to come to the mortuary with us to see if you can make an identification....'

PHILIP

I came out of the police station feeling as though I'd been punched in the middle, though no-one had laid a finger on me. I couldn't face the thought of going straight back to work so I went home.

I was in the kitchen filling the jug for coffee when I heard Christiane's voice from the bathroom.

'Is that you, Philip?'

'Yes, I've come home for an emergency cup of coffee.'

There was silence from the bathroom, but soon after Christiane appeared. She held her towel around her waist but was naked above.

'You'll have to excuse me but I've been playing squash. You aren't normally around at this hour so I left my clothes upstairs.'

She is quite flat-chested, and totally beautiful. Very lithe, too.

'Will you come and have a cup of coffee when you're ready? I need someone to talk to.'

She raised her eyebrows slightly, then went off to her room. Her movements were so graceful.

She'd held the towel quite low on her hips, and I'd noticed a red scar rising up her abdomen above the towel. An operation of some sort, that was still showing.

She came down a short while later, dressed but with her hair still wet.

'So what was so shocking? Not the sight of me half naked, I hope?'

'Absolutely not. It was a different body, actually. I've just come back from the main police station, and I've just identified a murder victim.'

'Merde…' She reached out, plunged the coffee pot and poured for both of us. She sat in silence, letting me start when I'd composed myself.

'You remember a little while ago I was complaining that I interviewed someone for a position, and then she'd disappeared when I tried to offer her the job. You may also remember the body that was found on the railway lines near Lancaster station a few weeks ago. You can probably see where I'm heading.'

'Oh God….' She put her hand to her mouth.

'The police were appealing for help to identify the body. I never thought there'd be any connection with my missing person, but I thought I'd just drop in and mention about her and when I described her it turned out that she was the woman. I've never felt so awful in my life before. They took me into the mortuary, and it was just like in the movies. They rolled out this long metal drawer, and it was her without a shadow of a doubt. They just showed me her face and her hands. When I interviewed her I noticed some distinctive scars on the back of her hand, and they were there. They tried to keep her neck covered, but I could see the top of some nasty marks there. The worst was that she had this awful clammy whiteness about her. I had to give them her address, and I guess they'll be going round to the house to see what they can find.

'It was a horrible experience – not just the body, but the questioning too. Every question almost sounds like an accusation the way they phrase it, even if you've got nothing to feel guilty about. The main guy asking the questions, Inspector Brady, was large and solid – looked pretty fit too. I wouldn't have liked to tangle with him, and I kept thinking he was viewing me as a suspect. The other guy, a Sergeant Nielsen, seemed a more reasonable sort of person. At least he didn't look like he was going to put the handcuffs on straight away.'

I stopped to drink some coffee. Christiane stayed silent.

'They kept asking me if I knew anything about her private life. They seemed to think I must have been to her house and might have known her well. I kept telling them I'd only ever met her once at the interview. In the end I was beginning to wonder if they had me down as a suspect.'

'What *were* you able to tell them about her?'

'I described the interview – not that there was a lot to say. I mentioned that once or twice she seemed a bit tense about questions, and that there seemed to be a couple of years in her life that weren't fully accounted for. But that isn't all that unusual – I've had it before. People have bits of their lives that they don't want to reveal. Broken marriages, domestic violence, divorces – that sort of thing. They asked me which questions she found difficult, but I couldn't remember that much detail. I've got to get my interview notes from work and take them in this afternoon, and sign a formal statement of identification at the same time.'

'What did she seem like as a person? The sort that something like this might happen to?'

'Absolutely not. I liked her. She seemed a genuinely pleasant person. A bit reserved. I had a sense that maybe she'd had a trauma in the past that she'd got over, but perhaps not quite. But she seemed a person that we'd be happy to employ, and when her references checked out okay I tried to offer her the job. Alas, too late.'

'The poor woman. The poor, poor woman.' Christiane seemed particularly distressed, but I was in a state to overreact myself.

We finished our coffee, and I went back to the university to get my notes on the interview.

PHILIP

Clutching my interview notes I headed for the Police Station where Sergeant Nielsen had said he'd meet me. We went into an interview room, again just like something on television. Spartan, not very well ventilated, and uncomfortable.

'Can I get you some tea or coffee or something?'

'I'm fine, thanks. What do you want me to do – just run through everything I wrote down?'

'Well, that'd be a good start, wouldn't it,' he said rather drily.

'Is it just the two of us?'

'Yep.'

'That's good. I found Inspector Brady a bit daunting this morning. I got the impression that he thought I was involved somehow.'

'Oh, you don't want to take much notice of that. He can be a bit full on, I grant you, but he's a good copper. Anyway, we have to keep all our options open, don't we?' There was a faint grin as he said that.

'Okay, first before an interview I look carefully through the

CV that they've sent. You can get a feel for the person from what they've written, though of course they can always get someone else to write it. Rosemary Mason's was quite good – nothing out of the ordinary, and she seemed to have had a reasonable work record.

'She lived originally in Preston. She got two A levels at school, then left to go and work in a grocery shop. After that she came to Lancaster and worked in the Council offices as a clerk. She got promoted to supervisor, then left to go to a big hardware firm where she was responsible for personnel management.

'Up to that point she was a clear and confident inter-viewee. Then suddenly, for the time about five years ago some vagueness crept in and she was clearly unwilling to talk about it. The work record in her application also didn't say much. I thought maybe she'd stopped to have children or something. I asked rather delicately if she was married, though I'm not supposed to do that. She didn't want to talk about it – she just said, rather tight-lipped – "I'm not married now". Then it crossed my mind that perhaps it was a marital break-up – I've had various people in interviews who don't want to talk about that, understandably.

'After the vague bit everything became more accurate again. She was still in Lancaster and she worked in an accounts office. She was a sort of general dogsbody as far as I could tell, but she filled in for various jobs and did well at them, and the firm gave her a very good reference. They said they were sorry to lose her. She left to go to a catering firm, where she supervised the ordering and managed a small number of staff. She did well at it, and that was ideal from our point of view so we were going to offer her our job. But then we couldn't find her.

'I haven't got any more notes than that, and I imagine that that doesn't give you much to go on.'

'Well, there's not a lot of meat there, I grant you. Still, there often isn't at first.'

'I will just say one more thing, which isn't in the notes because it was just my gut feeling. I'm quite used to people dodging questions or being evasive about certain things and I don't pay all that much attention to it, but with Ms Mason I felt it was a bit different. When we were talking about the bits she wanted to avoid she actually seemed a bit frightened by it all – not just embarrassed or dodging it.'

'Well, thank you for that, sir. Gut feelings by people who interview regularly can be quite accurate sometimes, though I don't know what to think of yours at this stage. I think our next job might be to search her house to see if we can pick anything up there. There is still one thing you could do for us if you don't mind – that's to give me the list of all her previous employers. You never know when one of them might have picked up something about her past which would give us a clue as to what's happened. I need to talk to them because they may have had particular gut feelings as well. Different people notice different things, so if you could give me the names I'd appreciate it.'

'No problem. The first one that I've got down was a grocery shop in Preston, where she first lived – it was Campbell and Fortescue in Market Street. Then she went to work at the Council offices in Lancaster as a clerk, and later as a supervisor. I can't tell you which part of the Council, I'm afraid, but they should have centralised records. After that she went to Advance Hardware as a personnel manager. I think that's that huge glass place at the entrance to the Garden Road Estate.

'Then there was the period where she became vaguer. After that, when she became more positive again, she was in Lancaster at Summit Engineering in the accounts office, though just as a general dogsbody as far as I could tell. Then in the end she went to Top-Flite Catering, where she supervised the ordering and managed a small number of staff. That was the experience that particularly attracted us to her, and they gave her a pretty good reference.'

'Thank you very much, sir – that's most helpful. I'll follow up on a few of those. Thank you very much for coming back in, and if there's anything else we'll be in touch. Oh, just before you go, Inspector Brady had one more question for you – what colour is your car?

'It's blue, why?'

'It wouldn't be an estate car, would it?'

'No, it's a saloon. It's a rather old Ford.'

'Thank you, sir. It's just that a white estate car was seen in the general vicinity of where the body was found, at roughly the right time, and we're trying to find out whose it might have been. So if it's any consolation, since it's blue I don't think Inspector Brady'll be banging you up any time soon...'

A slight wink as he said it helped.

SERGEANT NIELSEN

It was time for the routine work on Rosemary Mason. Check police and court records; check any other official records showing her doing anything; interview her neighbours, the postman, anyone else who might have known what sort of life she lived, who her associates were, and so on. Grinding and slow work, but you have to do it.

I'm certainly planning to interview some of her former work colleagues as well, having got the names of the companies from young Philip Dow. She could just have let slip to colleagues what she'd been worried about in the past.

I got Jimmy Garfield to do the neighbours. He's a bit new in the force, but he's bright and more importantly he gets on well with people. Somehow they feel confident with him and they tell him things that they mightn't tell others.

Especially Inspector Brady...

While Garfield was doing that, I did the official records and they were totally unrewarding. Rosemary Mason didn't appear to have had a car or a driving licence, so there weren't any traffic fines or related prosecutions. She had no record of any sort for crimes or misdemeanours. There was no record of a passport. She was registered as a ratepayer, and as a customer for electricity, gas and water. Apart from that there were no signs that she even existed.

I'd hoped that Jimmy would come back with something a bit more positive, but his face when he returned wasn't encouraging.

He told me that the next-door neighbours on either side said they virtually never saw Ms Mason. Occasional brief nods as she went to work or came home, but she was otherwise never outside, and her curtains were always drawn when she was in. She never invited people into her place, and if they invited her she always had an excuse for not coming. They didn't even ask after a while.

Various neighbours further along the street didn't even know that she existed.

He'd also bumped into the postman, who said that he almost never saw her, though he thought that when he did his rounds she was quite likely at work. He said he thought that she had very little mail, and what mail there was was all official – nothing personal. Though she got so little that he wasn't even sure of that.

Through the council Jimmy'd chased down one of the dustmen who did Merrington Road. The man didn't remember anything except that there was usually a bin out but it never had much in it. He didn't remember anything unusual being thrown out, though talking to him Jimmy'd felt that he didn't remember much in life anyway. Too much drinking, he thought.

Through the utilities he met with the meter readers who serviced Merrington Road, and like the dustman they had no comments. They didn't think they'd ever seen her when they'd read the meters, and they didn't think there was anything unusual about her usage of the services.

Rosemary Mason must have had an unbelievably quiet and dull life. I was almost ready to believe that she must have been a spy or master criminal, who was keeping a low profile in order to conduct a carefully concealed operation of some sort. But I don't think I'll float that one past Inspector Brady – I value my job a bit more than that.

I can't remember a time when this sort of checking provided so little – it's almost as though she wasn't a real person. It's all striking me as quite unusual, but I'm buggered if I know what to make of it.

* * *

I'd hoped to get something more positive from talking to the previous places where Rosemary Mason had worked, but the main thing that I achieved from that was an even bigger puzzle.

I decided to do them in reverse order, the most recent first, so I went to Top-Flite Catering. I was shown into the manager's office, and had to decline a wide assortment of new cakes and pastries that they were promoting. Some of them looked very nice, but I'd have big trouble with the wife if my waistline got any bigger than it already is. I did accept a coffee, though, and I quizzed the manager.

'Rosemary was an excellent worker, and we were very sad to lose her. She was not only good at her ordering work, but she was very good with staff. Everyone seemed to like her, and that's a real plus in a place like this.'

'You had a fair bit to do with her, sir?'

'I certainly did because she reported directly to me, and I always enjoyed our interactions. The only thing that surprised me was that she disappeared without saying goodbye to anyone or letting us know. We knew that she'd applied to the university because I had to write a reference for her, but we didn't know that she'd actually got the job. However, one day she simply didn't come in to work, and we never saw her again. That seemed very much out of character.'

'Well, sir, there was most unfortunately a reason for that. It hasn't been in the papers yet, but it'll be out soon so I can tell you. You would have heard about the murdered woman who was found on a railway lines several weeks ago – I'm sorry to have to say that that was Rosemary Mason.'

'Oh, bloody hell...'. He went quite pale. 'That's terrible. It never occurred to me in a fit of Sundays that that could have been Rosemary – you'd never have thought that something like that could happen to someone like her. Do you know what happened, and why?'

'We don't know a great deal at this stage, and that's why I'm talking to people like you in the hope of getting a better picture of her life. I don't suppose that in the light of this you've got any more thoughts to add?'

'I'm sorry but I don't. I can only say that she would have been about the last person to have something like that happen to her. I don't actually know much about her private life, but from what little she let drop it sounded as though it was pretty quiet. She didn't ever take time off for anything particular, and she didn't seem to go on holidays at all. Beyond that I can't think of anything.'

'Well, thank you, sir – it has given me a clearer picture of Ms Mason. If anything else crops up I can always get back to you.'

'Yes, you'd be most welcome. Oh hell, I'm going to have to get the staff together and tell them what had happened. If I'm allowed to do that at this stage of course?'

'I can't see why not, sir. It's going to be in the press pretty soon now. And good luck with doing it. I've had to do that sort of thing plenty of times in my career, and it never gets any easier.'

I left the manager still looking stunned, and went to Summit Engineering where I spoke to the accounts manager. He turned out to have been in the job and the company for only three months and he hadn't known Ms Mason. He called in an elderly accountant who'd been there for years, and I explained to him that I was looking for people's impressions of Rosemary Mason.

'I take it you've got a reason for coming to ask this?'

'I have, sir, and I'll tell you after I've heard any thoughts that you may have.'

'Well, firstly she was a good worker. She had to do all sorts of jobs in this office, and I never once heard her complain or say that it was beneath her. And whatever she did she did well. She was also very good with other staff – she was quiet, but she got on well with people. I suppose that she wasn't threatening in any way – that would have helped.'

'Did you get any idea of what sort of private life she might have led?'

He thought for a moment. 'I think the best answer to that

is that no, I didn't. I didn't at all, to an extent that was probably unusual. Most people at least talk a little about their interests and how they spend their time, but I don't remember her doing that at all. And one other comment – I thought that there was a slight air of sadness about her at times. Maybe something had happened in her past that was a bit traumatic, but I wouldn't be able to put any sort of finger on it.'

'Thank you very much, sir. There's certainly some food for thought there.' I then went on to tell him and the accounts manager about Ms Mason's murder, with the same shocked reaction as at the catering place. However, no further information came forward as a result of that news.

The remaining three places left me with a complete puzzle. I went to Advanced Hardware who seemed very efficient but said they'd never heard of anyone called Rosemary Mason. Very strange that a smart firm couldn't find someone they'd supposedly employed, so I asked them to check carefully through their records and they still couldn't find anyone with that name.

Then I went to Lancaster Council. I had trouble at first finding anyone who seemed to know anything at all, but I finally got someone with access to their staff files, and they said there wasn't one with that name. I asked to speak to someone who'd been in the council offices for a number of years, and they found a couple but neither could recall Rosemary's name. I didn't give that visit as much credence as the previous one because the council offices were very large and nobody seemed to take a great interest in anything, so I drove to Preston and called in at Campbell and Fortescue.

And unbelievably I had the same result there. Their staff

records were actually not complete because they'd had a fire at one time in the records office – a malfunctioning heater during the night, apparently. So they also had no record of her, but they were an old-fashioned grocer with a very personal touch, and they called in for me several staff who'd been there for many years, and not one of them remembered the name of Rosemary Mason.

By that time I was getting quite suspicious, and the first thought that crossed my mind was that there might have been some sort of scam going on. Maybe there was something dodgy in her past that had finally caught up with her, and that was why she was killed. The next thing would be to search her house – maybe some clues would turn up there if that was the case. It's quite difficult to cover your tracks completely if you're up to something.

PHILIP

A strange thing happened this morning. Christiane and I coincided in the kitchen mid-morning, and she was making coffee and offered me a cup. We were sitting at the table chatting about nothing in particular, when there was a loud and sharp knock on the front door.

It gave me a slight start, but that was nothing compared to Christiane's reaction. She looked shocked and turned white, shot up, almost ran to the back door and went out. A bit startled myself at this performance, I got up and went to the front door. It was the postman with a package for Christiane.

I took it back to the kitchen and drank some more coffee. Some moments later Christiane put her head round the door warily, then came in and went to her coffee.

'Are you okay?' I tried to say it as gently and neutrally as possible, because she obviously wasn't okay.

She sat in silence for a bit, looking down at the table. Then she spoke.

'I thought it was Giampaolo. I owe you a big apology because there's one part of my life I haven't told you about and it could affect you. I should never have come to stay here and exposed you to it.'

I probably looked a bit surprised since I was, but I said nothing because I thought more was coming. After another long pause, it did.

'I met Giampaolo Mellini while I was at Cambridge. He was exotic and exciting, and he seemed to think the same about me. Six months after we went down, we got married.'

She took a gulp of coffee.

'At first it was all fine. Then Paolo began to accuse me of being unfaithful and going with other men. It was completely untrue and I had no wish or need to do it anyway. He seemed to think he was inadequate sexually, which he wasn't, but I couldn't ever reassure him on that. I never gave him the slightest reason to think that I'd slept with other men, and I've never understood why he should even have thought that.

'Anyway, he became more extreme and wild in his accusations, and then began to get violent. When he was normal things were good and our relationship was quite passionate, but I could never quite relax, and gradually the bad times became more frequent.

'I thought that if we could start a family maybe things might get better, so I made the disastrous mistake of going off the pill but not telling Paolo. We still had sex at times and eventually I got pregnant. When I told Paolo he really lost it – as far as he was concerned that was confirmation that I was sleeping with other men. Why he should have thought the baby wasn't his I've no idea. It was. In all the time we were married I never went with another guy. Nor since as it happens.

'The pregnancy developed, and Paolo's jealousy along with

it. Then one day he came home in an absolute rage. He yelled at me, accused me of being a whore and God knows what else – I've blotted out the detail. He grabbed me, punched me, threw me to the ground and kicked me hard and many times in the stomach. I miscarried, got rushed to hospital, and had an operation that revealed a lot of damage. They fixed me up, but as a result I'll never get pregnant again.'

I heard all this with mounting horror. Instinctively I reached out to rest my hand on hers. She didn't respond, but neither did she remove hers.

'I'm desperately sorry to hear all of that – I had no idea. But how should that affect your living here?'

'The people at the hospital wanted me to press charges against Paolo, but I couldn't bring myself to do that. I had loved him deeply, and I still loved the person he was when he wasn't mad. But I didn't think we could stay living together so I left him. After a while I filed for divorce, and eventually it came through.

'Paolo wouldn't accept any of that. He hung around where I was living, he tried to break in, he harassed me in the street and at work. I took out restraining orders but he ignored them. I should have had him prosecuted, but I still couldn't bring myself to do that and ruin his life. Even though he was ruining mine.

'I fled to Exeter, but he tracked me down there after a while. Then I came up here – as quietly as I could – but I'm sure that sooner or later he'll find me here. If he finds me living in a house with another guy he'll become quite violent, and I shouldn't have exposed you to that. I should find somewhere else to live, where the owner won't be so compromised. He wouldn't have worried about Mrs Marshall in my old place, and she'd probably have hit him with a rolling pin or something if he'd tried anything on.'

It was my turn to remain silent for a bit, while my churning emotions simmered down. The chief emotion being anger. Finally I felt able to speak.

'Christiane, I'm devastated on your behalf to hear all of this, but I can't see the slightest reason why you should move from here. In fact I'd be greatly upset if you did. I've never liked bullying, which is what this is. This is my house, and others can't dictate who lives here and who doesn't. That may sound arrogant but it isn't meant to be – I just don't think ex-husbands have a right to determine that. And if you don't want to listen to my view, listen to Aunt Clarissa's. She'd be hugely disappointed if you let a bullying male drive you out of her house. She chained herself to railings for years to take on bullies and unfairness, and she'd be right back on the railings for this one. Or defending you with a flailing walking stick or something. Please, please stay for her.'

Christiane looked at me for the first time since she started her story.

'Thank you, Philip' was all she said, but the eyes said a bit more.

'I have no worries,' I said. 'If Giampaolo turns up here, I'll cope.' Which was optimistic as it turned out, but I didn't know it at the time.

FRANK ELLIOTT

Some mornings go better than others. Today I confirmed that a mouse infestation in Cartland Ward was completely gone. I shouldn't have been too surprised, though, because mice are the easiest of my pests to control. They're highly inquisitive and they go for the baits every time. And the baits still work well with them.

I wish I could say the same for rats. I've learnt to have the greatest respect for rats – they're some of the smartest animals around when it comes to survival. They're highly wary of anything new, and much of the time they just ignore any baits I put out. It doesn't help that in a mental hospital there's often a lot of loose food around the place one way or another, so they don't have to take my offerings because they're starving. They're also becoming resistant to some of the baits.

A few years back our management sent me on a course to learn rat psychology and how to control the little buggers, but I reckon the rats went on a parallel course at the same time on how to outsmart humans. And theirs were the better course.

As I came out of Cartland I bumped into the person who I

think's the saddest case in the whole hospital. Aggie Ransome's an old lady now. She's been here most of her adult life, and the awful thing is that she never had any mental problem. The lady who runs the sewing room told me that when Aggie were little she were interfered with by her uncle, and she were then declared to be morally defective and placed into the institution to get her out of the way. I can't imagine a worse fate than to be punished wi' a life in here for something that weren't even your fault. And that happened in what my parents used to call the good old days.

Although she's old now she still has good looks. Her face may have gone quite wrinkled, but she would have been a beauty when she was young, and she has the most beautiful white hair. You can see why she would have attracted men when she was young, and it's so tragic that her uncle spoiled it all for her.

I always give a cheerful hello to Aggie, and the reaction varies. On a bad day she just ignores you. Most of the time you just get a grunt, but it's not unfriendly. Today I got a brief "Morning", so it must have been a good day. No smile, but I don't think I've ever seen her smile. Which I can understand, of course.

Aggie's the only patient that I knew that sort of story about, but one of the older ladies in the sewing room told me that there were all sorts of things in the earlier days that were wrong. A husband who got tired of his wife would get a friendly doctor to have her declared mentally deficient, and then she were banged up in here while her husband went off wi' a new totty. In some cases the wife was having a bad case of post-natal depression, I think they call it, and she were put in here for that. And once you were in here it was hard to get out again. Others were alcoholics, and the family couldn't cope with 'em – or didn't want to try.

Aggie'd made me feel a bit more cheerful as I headed off to a report of cockroaches in Harding Ward. They're another pest that's difficult to control in a mental hospital – they go for the same thrown away food as the rats do. They do take my baits and some of 'em do die, but there's so many of 'em that I sometimes think it's a drop in the ocean. Still, you've got to try. It's a lot easier in the University computer centre, which is pretty neat and tidy all the time. My mate Christina makes sure of that.

CHRISTIANE

Philip's gone to a meeting in Newcastle for two days, and I'm going to do something completely out of character, of which I totally disapprove. I'm going to snoop in his bedroom.

In my defence, I do have a reason. I find Philip a total enigma as a person. He looks to all intents and purposes like a normal human being, and acts it for much of the time, but there just seems to be part of a personality lacking. He can seem a bit like a robot, or a tailor's dummy come to life. He doesn't appear to have any particular friends – at least nobody comes round here, and he doesn't go out much at all except for work. It spooks me a bit – if I can't understand what sort of a person he is, it's rather unnerving.

He also seems to have no sex life of any sort. I refuse to believe that anyone under the age of about eighty doesn't have some sort of sexual activity, but I get no clue at all about Philip's. He had that story one time about a Malaysian girlfriend, which may or may not have been true, but there's been no female visiting him here since I've been here and he doesn't go out often enough to have a regular liaison anywhere else. He's also not shown any interest in me, though given my history that doesn't surprise me.

I'd initially thought he might have been gay, but again there's no sign of a boyfriend anywhere. It worries me that that leaves pornography as a possibility, and that's what I'd like to check out. I'd feel very uncomfortable living here if my landlord – if you can call him that – is a serial pornographer. Especially paedophilia or something like that. I'd definitely look for somewhere else to go, despite the advantages of this place.

So here I am in Philip's bedroom, looking around.

The most obvious place is a large and heavy wardrobe in the corner, so I open that carefully. It's quite neat inside, but there's a small pile of magazines in one corner. I pick them up carefully.

The top one turns out to have photos of nude women in it. However, it's National Geographic and the nudes are Amazon jungle dwellers doing their natural thing, and they're about as unerotic as any nudes can be. That copy had probably been kept because there were also some amazing pictures of the Great Barrier Reef, which was the main feature of the issue. The rest of the heap was National Geographic too.

I put the magazines back, and bend down to the space under the bed. There's some dust there, and three pairs of shoes and a small cardboard box. I lift the box out very carefully because I'll have to replace it in its dust profile, and I take off the lid. It contains various keys, which from the labels are spares to various doors of the house. I put the box back carefully, and I don't think anyone would notice that it's been disturbed.

I also put my hand gently between the mattress and the bed

base, in case anything has been stuffed in there. There's nothing in any of the parts that I can reach.

What next? There's a chest of drawers that seems a possibility. I open each drawer in turn and rummage very gently under things without disturbing the general pattern. Philip is obviously quite a neat storer, so it isn't hard to do. There are assorted clothes, but no magazines and nothing overtly sexual. No feminine underwear or anything like that.

That only leaves the bedside cabinet. The cupboard at the bottom doesn't contain a chamber pot like some do – it's hardly got anything. A worn pair of bedroom slippers, a shoe-horn and what looks like an old chest-expander, which from the amount of dust on it doesn't seem to have been used for a long while.

There's also a drawer which I open carefully. It contains a jumble of bits and pieces, including five unused condoms in foil packs. In addition there's also a small pile of photos at the back of the drawer, face down.

I pull them out. The first one is of a naked female. She's short and dumpy, has small, conical breasts, and looks Asian. She's facing the camera, and the most remarkable thing about her is her challenging expression. No modesty – just a full-on challenge to the photographer to disapprove in any way.

In the second picture the same female is on her hands and knees. Her breasts hang down as much as their small size permits, and again she's glaring at the camera.

In the third picture she's lying on her back on a bed. The photographer was standing at her feet, and she has her legs wide open in a most unedifying pose that leaves nothing to the imagination. And you guessed it – she was daring the photographer to disapprove.

The fourth picture is of Philip, lying naked on a bed and with an erection. He at least had the grace to look embarrassed.

I put the photos back as I'd found them. They could be classified as dirty pictures, but they were obviously private records of a relationship which didn't make them pornography in the usual sense. How anyone could find them appealing or want to keep them I couldn't imagine, but then they weren't mine. I presume the female was the Lucy he'd spoken about earlier. I'd imagined someone a bit more glamorous.

So my search was ended and I hadn't really found anything. There was still his computer, but there was no way I was going to be stupid enough to try to get into that. He could be spending all his time surfing for pornography there – I don't know. There were the pictures of the one girlfriend, so I guess I have to give him the benefit of the doubt.

I was no further forward in understanding Philip as a person, and I felt sullied by the whole process. The pictures were sordid, but it was my fault that I'd seen them. I'd gone against all my principles in making the search and it hadn't helped me. My mother always said no good ever came of snooping, and I'd just proved her right.

Yeuch.

PHILIP

I'd taken the afternoon off after my trip to Newcastle, and I was sitting in the front room doing a crossword when there was a sudden pounding on the back door. This was odd because the backyard only opens into a narrow lane. Garbage trucks come along the lane but almost nobody else uses it, and nobody ever comes to our back door. The back gate's locked, anyway.

I opened the door and Christiane staggered in. Her hair was dishevelled and her face pale, and she'd scraped some skin off both legs. There was a dirty streak across her shorts, and a small rip at the front.

'Christiane, what on earth's happened to you?'

'I was walking home, and just where the little footpath runs through from our street to the back lane a car in the street suddenly did a U-turn and came to a sharp stop beside me. I looked at the driver and I'm sure it was Paolo. I panicked and rushed down the footpath and along the back lane until I saw our backyard, and I scrambled over the top of the fence and dropped into the yard. Then I crawled into the alcove where the rubbish bins are stored and hid there.

'The car couldn't follow me down the little footpath, but he must have found the end of the lane because a car came slowly cruising down the laneway a couple of minutes later, obviously looking for something. However, he couldn't have known which yard I might have been in, and eventually he went away. But it means that he probably knows now at least roughly where I'm living. It still worries me that I'm exposing you to possible trouble with him.'

'Christiane, please don't worry about that in the slightest. I'm appalled by this sort of behaviour, and we're certainly not giving in to it. But I'm worried by you – you look pretty white. You're obviously in shock. Come in and sit down in the front room, and I'll give you some remedial treatment.'

I sat her down in the most comfortable chair – she more or less collapsed into it – and I put on a CD of Alfred Deller singing Couperin's "Leçons de Ténèbres". In my view that's one of the most soothing pieces of music that you can get. The gentle, balmy voice drifted peacefully through the room. I left her in a rather catatonic state and went to get some medication. I poured a moderate sized dose and passed it to her. She looked at it rather doubtfully, then took a sip and gasped, then another sip. After a moment she said:

'That's rather nice. What is it?'

'It's Caol Ila whisky. It's a single malt from Islay in Scotland. A friend who knew something about whiskies told me about it, and I keep a bottle in the cupboard for special occasions. Or medication purposes when required. I rather like it too, and I seem to need medication every now and then. Now just sit there and I'll go and get some antiseptic.'

'I'll be all right, really.' She made as though to get up, but was having difficulty.

'May I ask you, very politely, to shut up and sit still while I go and get ready to practice my home nursing. I promise you it won't do you any harm, and it might just help. You've scraped both legs, which you must have done on the top of the fence, and I shudder to think what horrible organisms might have been growing there.'

I got a small bowl and a bit of salt from the kitchen, and some antiseptic and soft cloths from the bathroom. I debated whether to use cold or tepid water, but decided that cold might be a bit of a shock on the grazes so I got tepid and mixed the salt and antiseptic in.

I went back and knelt beside Christiane, and bathed her left shin which was well scraped – then the inside of her right thigh which had some unpleasant and dirty scratches. I swabbed it all gently with the wet cloth, and then patted it dry with a clean, soft one. I hoped this was what home nurses were supposed to do. It didn't seem to be doing any harm, anyway.

The scrapes weren't as deep as I'd first feared, and both looked a lot better after the treatment.

'Neither of these are bleeding or oozing much. I can dress them if you like but it might be better if they stayed exposed to the air to heal faster. But I've got dressings and bandages in the bathroom any time you want them or need them.'

Christiane just nodded, but she obviously wasn't with it and she just stayed sitting in the chair in a sort of daze. I thought I'd better keep an eye on her for a bit, so I got a crossword and sat in one of the other chairs. She dozed off for a bit because the CD finished and she didn't stir, so I got up and put on another one of music by Hildegard von Bingen. Another one that relaxes the spirit wonderfully. Eventually she woke up, and she had a rather better colour than before.

'Thank you so much for coping with me like this. I do feel a bit better now.'

'That's good. My nursing can't have been too much of a disaster then. Look, I've just noticed that it's lunchtime – can I get you something to eat before you go and bath or whatever?'

She hesitated. 'I don't feel all that much like bread...'

'How about a light omelette, then? I can have one ready in about eight minutes. Ten max.'

'That would actually be rather nice. Thank you.'

'Well, come and sit in the kitchen so I can keep an eye on you, and I'll get started.' I didn't trust her not to go wandering off upstairs if I couldn't see her, and she'd probably have fallen or something and done even more harm.

She came into the kitchen and flopped on to one of the chairs. I put two plates in the oven, then got six eggs out of the fridge and whipped them up with a tiny bit of milk and a small dob of butter. Then a sprinkling of mild paprika, and I went out to get two sprigs of thyme from the backyard. I stripped the tiny leaves from the thyme into the mixture and whipped it again. Then a large frying pan with a little oil, very hot, and in with half the mixture.

I swirled it all round the pan where it began to set quickly. I folded it over while it was still slightly wet on top, and popped it on a plate in the oven. Then repeated the process, and gave Christiane the second one because it was more freshly cooked. I felt quite professional – not sure how it looked to her, though.

We ate in silence and then she said: 'This is actually rather good. Where did you learn to cook omelettes like that?'

'You'll laugh, but it was from a TV programme. There was a well-known chef, I can't remember who now, who was running through various basic cooking techniques, and I thought I ought to learn a few. A lot of them were ones that didn't appeal greatly, or I thought I'd never manage them, but the omelette one seemed straightforward and I've always liked omelettes. I'm glad you thought it was okay.'

'It's more than okay, it's delicious. You've got some extra flavours in there I think? I wasn't really watching as you did it.'

'A small amount of paprika – not the hot one – but the bit that really makes it is a few leaves off a sprig of your thyme in the backyard – the plant that you bought the other day. I hoped you wouldn't mind me using a little bit in the interests of edibility.'

'Philip, of course I don't mind, and anyway it's not my thyme, it's ours. I use your herbs, so you use mine. They're ours!'

Which was a nice thought. Christiane was looking a bit stronger now, but she needed to go and bath.

'Don't you worry about washing up or anything – I'll do this. You go and get yourself organised again.'

'Thank you so much. Now that I look at myself I think I'd better go and have a bath – I seem to be pretty dirty. And I need to change my clothes – they're dirty as well as torn.'

'My pleasure – I was just glad to be here when this happened. But be a bit careful in the bath with the scratches – don't rub them open or anything. And please just let me know if there's anything more I can do. Really...'

She just nodded, and went upstairs to undress.

CHRISTIANE

I felt I needed something a bit special after today's shock, so I put some of the last bath salts that my mother had given me a while ago into the bath. They had a beautiful fragrance that I couldn't pin down, and they were wonderfully relaxing.

I lay in the warm bath with all sorts of thoughts churning through my mind. It would be lovely to stay in the bath forever. I'd hoped that I might have escaped from Giampaolo, though I'd always known that that was a forlorn hope. The whole awful circus is repeating itself again, and this time I've involved an innocent party with Philip.

And he'd been very kind to me when I came in in such a mess. He was very calming, and his choice of music was perfect. He'd never given any indication that he had interests of that sort. I must look through his collection of CDs a bit more carefully.

The whisky was very welcome too. I've only had rather ordinary whiskies before and never taken to them. However, after that one I think I could be converted.

I pondered for ages on whether or not I should leave and try to find yet another sanctuary somewhere, but short of a nunnery that doesn't seem likely. And Philip had said very clearly that he didn't want me to give in to Giampaolo's bullying, and he'd cope if necessary.

I don't think he quite knows what he might be in for, but the clincher is Great Great Aunt Clarissa. She'd most certainly not have approved of me giving in, and if she was strong enough to stand up for her principles I should be too. Us women have to stick together.

And if there was one positive out of what happened it was a lovely feeling of being completely looked after. When I was little and I damaged myself, my mother was always there and I could just surrender myself to her and know she'd do all the right things to make me better. I haven't ever felt like that since my early teens, but today it happened again. Not really by choice, but I just felt paralysed by the shock and I let Philip do it all. It was lovely to drop back into childhood for a few minutes, and I owe him for that.

And of all people it was Philip. It makes his character all the more puzzling in that suddenly he stopped being robotic or zombie-like and became a real, animated human being. Not to mention revealing himself as an omelette cook, which was surprising. So it can happen, and he just needs to do it more often. But what – other than being faced with a medical emergency, which I very much hope not to repeat – switches that side of him on? The mystery remains.

AGGIE RANSOME

It could never be like home, but over time I got used to this hospital. The people here aren't nutters mostly – they're what my parents used to call "simple". I know in my heart I'm not one of them, but nobody ever gave me the chance to explain.

I mightn't have survived if it hadn't been for one kind nurse who was responsible for me at the start. I think she must have been given the story of what happened, and she was smart enough to work out what had really happened. She never said, and I don't suppose she could have done anything about it, but she was very kind to me. She talked to me a lot, and she treated me as though I was normal which some didn't.

She got me to help her with various little jobs. At first I thought she was just trying to save herself some work, but later on I realised that she was giving me a place in the hospital, and some dignity again. And this is how I've been in all these later years. I potter from ward to ward, do a bit of cleaning, empty the wastepaper baskets, fetch a few supplies, and things like that. Most of the ward staff have a cheery word for me. It's like a little community, and I can feel I'm a member of that.

I even talk to some of the nicer patients, and I've come to realise that some of them have been dumped by their families just like me. In some cases it might have been that the families couldn't look after them, but in others I know that the family simply couldn't be bothered. Or they were too embarrassed to let the neighbours see their simple child. I've always felt a special sympathy for them, even when I've understood that they'd have been a handful.

But I've never forgiven Uncle Bertie for taking my life away from me. I don't know if he's still alive, but if God does exist I hope he's managed to strike Uncle Bertie down. Horribly, too. I hate my uncle as deeply now as I did the day I was sent away. He should rot in hell.

PHILIP

It was almost a replay of that earlier day when Christiane had told me about her problems with Giampaolo. We were once more sitting together at the kitchen table having a casual cup of coffee – it was becoming a habit – when there was a sharp sound of the door knocker. Christiane went white again, and headed towards the back door.

I went to the front. I was sure it was the postman once more, but a sixth sense was telling me that maybe this time it wasn't. However, the sixth sense wasn't fast enough to save me.

I opened the door to see not the postman but somebody I was fairly sure must be Giampaolo. But even as it registered, he yelled 'Where is the bitch?', lunged forward and gave me a hard shove in the chest. I stepped backwards to regain my balance, but I caught my foot against the step in the hallway. I flailed my arms out behind me to grab something and recover my footing, but I couldn't. I think I must have wedged my left arm down the umbrella hole in the hall stand, and after that it's a blur. I remember a violent pain in my arm, a splintering sound, timber crashing all around me and hitting various bits of me, another pain in my right arm, and then blackness.

* * *

I was vaguely aware of a stretcher and an ambulance man, but the next thing I remember clearly is lying in a hospital bed, and various bits of me hurt. My left arm had a bit of plaster on it and my right arm had a bandage and a sling.

I lay in a rather dazed state for a while, and then as consciousness became sharper and the background came into focus I could see beds, screens and a lot of white and chrome surfaces that suggested "hospital".

As the focus became a bit clearer I could see figures, and one of them turned out to be Christiane near the ward door talking to a large and cheerful black nurse. The nurse seemed to be nodding a lot.

The nurse must have noticed that I was awake, because she said something to Christiane and nodded at me. Christiane came over and sat down beside me, putting her hand lightly on my bandaged arm. It was a featherlight touch, but it was very nice.

'I believe you met Giampaolo?'

'I did. I told you earlier that if it happened I'd cope, but I didn't. What happened? I hope he didn't get you too?'

'No, I escaped, thanks in part to Aunt Clarissa. I don't know what did happen, but you were found unconscious in the wreckage of the hall stand, which had become a sort of barricade in the hallway. I think Paolo must eventually have climbed over it, but it slowed him down enough for me to get well away.'

'I ran round next door, and the neighbour called the police and ambulance. I knew it was Paolo because I heard him yell at you, and I heard crashing so I thought there might have been some injury. I'm sorry I was too much of a coward to come round and rescue you – the neighbour one house up from us did that. And I'm sorry that you got so involved in my problems, and I'm really sorry about Aunt Clarissa's hall stand.'

She took her hand away again.

'Don't be sorry – none of it's your fault, and I think it's just as well that you did stay out of the way – it might all have been far worse. I'll get over it. I should have been able to look after myself better but he took me by surprise. He pushed me backwards and I tripped against the hall step and lost my balance. And don't worry about the hall stand. It wouldn't have survived another move, and I think Aunt Clarissa would have approved of its use against Giampaolo. I hope it hit the bastard as well as me.'

'I believe there was blood on one of the upper parts, and the police thought that that bit couldn't have hit you. Though looking at the bruises on you, various bits of it did hit you too. Anyway, the police have taken the remains away for DNA testing which should sort out whose blood is which. How are you feeling, anyway?'

'A number of bits of me are rather sore, as you've obviously seen, but apart from that I don't feel too bad. I saw you talking to the nurse – d'you know what they're going to do with me?'

'That was Sister Sullivan, who's been looking after you. She says you have a break in your left arm – fortunately not a major one – and you've sprained your right wrist. You also had concussion, and you've got some bruising on various parts of you.

Apart from the concussion you're okay now, if you can call this okay. They'd be prepared to release you if there's someone at home to keep an eye on you for a day or two, but they haven't got anyone for the home care that you'd need because you can't wash yourself.'

She gave me a quick look. 'I said to Sister Sullivan that I could probably do that. It's the least I can do for you after my ex beat you up, and you looked after me the other day. I didn't think you'd want to stay in hospital any longer than you had to.'

'You're right about that – I'm not mad keen on these places. But I wouldn't want to be a problem for you. Are you sure it'd be okay?'

'Can't see why not. I'll go and see Sister.'

Sister Sullivan was happy, so they discharged me. We went home by taxi. The hallway looked bare – the police must have removed the whole hallstand as evidence – and the wall was gouged a bit, but it was actually better without the monstrosity to look at. And it had gone out in a final moment of glory. I think Aunt Clarissa would actually have been proud of it.

The next hurdle would be learning how not to let a broken arm stuff me up too much – and being bathed by my tenant. Ordinarily that wouldn't have bothered me at all, but it was a bit different given my feelings for this particular nurse. I guess it'll be all right on the day....

CHRISTIANE

It was bath time for Philip, and I was beginning to doubt whether I should have offered to bath him at all without even asking. He might have some embarrassing condition or something – some people do. Still, I imagine he'd rather feel clean, and there wasn't much choice because Sister Sullivan didn't have anyone else available. He'd probably have had a female nurse doing it in the hospital anyway, though an anonymous nurse mightn't have been as embarrassing as a tenant that you're stuck with.

We'd agreed to do the bath late in the evening so I didn't have the tedious chore of re-fastening all his clothes, which have to be pinned together rather intricately. I went to Philip.

'Bath now, okay? I'll go and run it and then get you.'

He nodded, but he didn't sound very enthusiastic.

I went to the bathroom, laid out bathmat, towel and face-flannel, and started running the bath. Halfway through it occurred to me that he would probably be a bit clumsy, strapped up as he was, and I was likely to get wet during this process so I went and changed into a T-shirt and gym shorts.

I tried dipping my elbow in the bath like I'd seen people do in films, but that didn't seem a good test so I just stuck my hand into the water. When I thought it was the right temperature and full enough I went and got Philip.

'Stand here and I'll undress you.'

Still no enthusiasm. Well, stuff him if he doesn't want to. He needs to get washed.

Because of his plastered and slung arms we'd had to pin a shirt around him, and cut an old pullover to go over the top. I took his shoes and socks off, unpinned the pullover and shirt, then took off his trousers, then the vest that we'd also pinned round him, and finally his underpants.

Standing completely naked apart from the plaster, it was obvious that he didn't have any embarrassing conditions, so I don't know why he was acting so childishly. The only surprising thing about him was that he was rather hairless for a male, though that was partly in contrast to my ex Giampaolo. Paolo could have given any gorilla a run for its money in the hair stakes. He had a thick mat of black hair all over his chest and abdomen, and over his shoulders and halfway down his back. Philip had some wispy areas on his sternum, and some fine downy hair on his arms, and not much else on his body apart from some sparse pubic hair. Even I could do better in that regard. Still, if you don't have it you don't have it, and Paolo was quite gross that way.

Philip did have quite a good figure though, which you wouldn't think from the awful clothing he always wears. Well-muscled and flat-stomached, he stands quite straight. If he'd dress better he wouldn't look too bad. His usual outfits are the sort of thing that a mother would choose for a schoolboy.

'Hop into the bath, hold up your arms and rest them on mine so they don't get the plaster wet, and I'll lower you into the water.'

I was worried that he'd slip and hurt himself even more, but he got down okay and I sloshed water all over him.

'You look like something from "Curse of the Mummy's Tomb", but a bit more animated. A bit…. Now get up and I'll soap you all over.'

Which I did, with more copious lather than I'd intended. I was getting it all over me too and I was glad I'd changed.

When I got to the nether regions he went even pinker than the temperature of the water could account for, and said 'I'm sorry you have to do this for me.'

'Oh, for God's sake, Philip – we're only humans. If Sister Sullivan can do this, so can I.'

I rinsed him off, soaking myself further in the process. Finally I got him dried off. 'Do I need to get you some pyjamas?'

He went pink again. 'I don't wear them so you don't need to fetch any,' he muttered.

I was getting cross with all this unnecessary modesty, but I just rolled my eyes.

He thanked me rather formally and went off to bed. I stayed to clean up the bathroom, and I noticed in the mirror that I'd got about as wet as he had.

I'd thought before we started that maybe bathing someone else would be a bit of a hoot, but it all fell quite flat. Well, stuff him. All I could think of then was to go to bed myself.

I lay in bed looking at the stars through the ceiling window. The sky was beautiful, but I couldn't get off to sleep.

PHILIP

Life just doesn't work out. I'd wanted nothing more than some sort of intimate contact with Christiane, and when it happened I'd made it a total non-event. I'd behaved like a little boy, and she must have thought I was even more of an idiot than I seemed before.

I was coming to the conclusion that I'm a failure in any sort of human relations when I heard a slight creak of the stairs. Presumably Christiane coming down to the toilet. I listened for the usual squeak of the toilet door, which needs a bit of oil on its hinges, but it didn't come. In fact nothing came for a moment or two; then I heard a soft voice at the door say 'Philip?'. So soft I almost wondered if I'd imagined it.

'Yes?' My heart was suddenly in my mouth.

A moment more silence, then 'It's very quiet and lonely upstairs...'

'I was lying here thinking how quiet and lonely it is down here too.' And I lifted the bedsheet with my better arm.

She came into the bed, and I discovered that she was naked

too. I thought of a hundred things to say, and decided to say none of them.

She nestled against me, and after a while said: 'I haven't had any intimate contact with another person since Paolo left me. I thought I was okay with that, but after touching you in the bath tonight, for the first time I felt very lonely. I think I need another body just to hold and snuggle against.'

'It's been a long time for me too...'

We nestled for a while, as much as I was able to do with my strapping, and then she said: 'I'm sorry if you didn't really want me in here.'

'Christiane – I've dreamed about this ever since I first saw you. And it's just come true.'

She pulled back a little at that. 'You haven't ever given the slightest sign of that since I've been living here, or made a pass at me or anything. I thought you must be quite uninterested.'

'I've been agonising over whether or not to show my feelings ever since you moved in here, but I thought it would frighten you away if I did. I remember the many glamorous men you went out with at uni, and I know I'm not in that league. I'd rather have you here and unavailable than gone altogether.'

'Well, you're a wimp, Philip.' But she said it not too unkindly. 'Remember the saying "Faint heart ne'er won fair lady".'

'And I also remember the saying "Better a bird in the flat than any number out there in the rest of Lancaster".'

'And I'll retaliate with: "Nothing ventured, nothing gained".'

'And I'll give you one good reason back. Three times in my life I've been very keen on a girl and wanted to take a relationship further, and each time the response was "Oh, you're a nice enough person but I'm looking for someone a bit more interesting", or "someone with more character", or something like that. It becomes very hurtful after a while, and you don't feel like doing it again. And then the class vote for me as the year's most boring just seemed to confirm that.'

There was silence for a bit, and then Christiane said: 'I've never understood why men seem to find me attractive. I'm flat-chested. I don't have good hips – my figure's more like a boy's. I'm not beautiful like in classical portraits. All the things that men like, and I don't have any of them.'

How far wrong could anyone be...?

'And yet lots of men at Cambridge were attracted to you, which shows that everything you've just listed is completely irrelevant. What you have is something special that goes way beyond any of those things. It's a rare quality that people have been trying to put a name to since language was invented. I don't think anyone's succeeded yet, and I certainly can't. It's an aura rather than physical characteristics, and it's the person not the body. I wish I could explain it better but I can't. All I can say is - have you ever seen any films with Audrey Hepburn in them?'

'Quite a while ago, but yes.'

'Well, she's one person I can think of who had that same sort of appeal. She only had to turn her wide eyes on to any male and smile her mysterious smile, and he just melted. She had a boyish figure and smallish breasts, and that was entirely unimportant. She was beautiful and fascinating and attractive.'

Christiane was silent for a moment, then said: 'I'm damaged goods now, though.'

'Christiane, you're being completely irrelevant again. You're still the same beautiful human being. It doesn't change the person you are in the slightest. Please tell me you won't ever say that again.'

She didn't say anything, and I could only hope that the thought sank in. After a bit she said: 'But you're still a wimp, though.'

'Well, I have it on good authority that I'm totally boring. Why would any woman with a choice in the matter even look at someone like me?'

'Now it's my turn to tell you never to say anything like that again. That sort of thinking does make you boring. In point of fact, I don't think you are boring – you're maybe too quiet and too retiring, but not boring. You're interested in all sorts of food, music if your CDs are anything to go by, travel to exotic locations and so on, and that's certainly not boring. I don't actually know why you got the vote, because there were far more boring people in the class than you. Do you remember that Nigel something with the floppy fair hair? He spent all his time telling everyone how wonderful he was. Now that really was boring.'

I murmured 'Fig Jam.'

'What's jam got to do with it?'

'Fig Jam. Fuck, I'm Good – Just Ask Me. Sorry, bit rude.'

'Oh, right – well that certainly does sum him up. And there were others. There was Randolph, who called himself Randy and thought he was God's gift to the female gender. He had a big cock, and he thought that was all there was to it. I can tell you from experience that he was a great disappointment, and I know the other girls in the class thought the same. He was a bore telling us all the time how good he was in the cot.'

I knew that Christiane had had a pretty active love life as a student, but I didn't really want to know details like that.

Then we seemed to run out of words, and we switched to some more snuggling. It was really all we could do with me strapped up as I was...

* * *

Just before dawn we were woken by the first bus of the morning. I hear them every day. The loud gear change as they reach the top of the hill and turn towards the house, then the louder roar of the engine as they accelerate along the road.

I said: 'There are some disadvantages to this room. I think I probably should have let this one rather than the top floor. I'm sure you don't get all that noise up in your place in the sky.'

'It's true, I don't. But there are a few compensations down here. One or two....' And she snuggled closer to me again.

PHILIP

The unreal night had passed, and life was becoming a bit more normal. I'd also recovered somewhat and was beginning to feel more human again, though I did panic a bit when there was another sharp knock on the door. Christiane was out, and I twitched nearly as much as she would have done. However, I wasn't going to be cowed by anything so I went to answer it.

It was Sergeant Nielsen again.

'It's all right, sir – I haven't come to arrest you. Yet...' Another slight wink, which was a relief. 'In fact it isn't to do with the dead lady at all. We had a report from the hospital that you were assaulted the other day, and I wondered if you'd like to tell me a bit more about it.' He nodded at my strapping. 'I can see you did have a bit of a run-in.'

'Yes, I'm currently sharing this house with a female, and it was her ex-husband who did this. And before you ask, no, we don't have any sort of relationship other than landlord and tenant.' Well, that was still more or less true. 'I've never given the ex the slightest reason to assault me. However, I gather that he has something of a history of this sort of thing. My tenant currently has an order out against him, but that doesn't seem to stop him. I believe he assaulted her quite violently on one occasion.'

Christiane probably wouldn't have wanted me to go into all of this, but I was feeling that enough was enough and Paolo needed to be stopped. You can feel quite bilious when you're still in some pain.

'So would you like to tell me what happened, sir?'

'Quite simple, really. I heard a knock on the door and I thought it was probably the postman. When I opened it I saw a male who I've never seen before. He said "Where is the bitch?", or something like that, stepped forward and punched me hard in the chest. I stepped back and caught the step just behind me. I lunged out backwards to try to get my balance, but apparently I tripped and fell into the hall stand that was inside the door. My arm was trapped, and I went backwards with the sound of massive splintering. After that I don't remember anything until I came to in the hospital.'

'That sounds like a clear offence to me. Do you know if there were any witnesses at all?'

'I don't know if anyone saw the actual assault, but I heard afterwards that the neighbour one house up heard the noise and came round to see what was happening. I believe the offender went upstairs looking for my tenant after he'd knocked me out, and the neighbour might have seen him because I was told that she came round quite quickly to see what had happened. The neighbour was also the one who called the ambulance, and the ambulance driver may have seen something – I don't know.'

'Thanks. We've already spoken to the ambulance man and

the hospital, but they couldn't say much more than the fact that you were injured and it obviously wasn't accidental. However, I might interview the neighbour after this if she's in. What about your tenant – she wasn't home at the time?'

'The honest answer to that is that she was home until she heard the doorknock, and then she shot out of the back door as fast as possible. She said afterwards that she suspected it might have been the ex and she knew what to expect. Which I think tells you even more about him.'

'It does rather. Can you give me a description of the offender?'

'Not a very good one, I'm afraid. It all happened so quickly that I didn't register all that much while I was still conscious. He was slightly taller than me, and more solidly built. He had almost black hair – also a snarling expression, which won't be much help to you.'

'No, we might pass on that one. Anyway, an offence was clearly committed. Would you like to tell me whether or not you want to lay charges, or at least have the matter pursued further?'

'Most certainly I would. You can't have people going around feeling that they can do this sort of thing, and from all accounts he's a serial offender. I also believe that my tenant has a right to live her life in peace. And he caused the destruction of a valuable antique hall stand. Well, maybe forget the valuable, but it was old and it was quite a useful hall stand.'

'Good for you, sir – I'll follow it up further now.'

'While you're here, have you made any progress on the other matter that you spoke to me about?'

'I wish I could say yes, sir, but it'd be stretching the truth.

We've had a preliminary look through Ms Mason's house, but it was pretty uninformative I'd have to say. We're working on it further now.'

'Okay, thanks, and good luck. I'll keep thinking and see if I can remember anything else that might be of use.'

'I might just mention one other thing as well. I went to chase up Ms Mason's previous workplaces to see if anyone there knew why she mightn't have wanted to talk about her previous employments. The latest two said there was no problem of any sort – she was really good, but the earlier ones said that she'd never worked for them. They didn't know her name at all, and she wasn't in their staff files. It sounds as though there's something a bit suss there, but I'm buggered if I can guess what it might be.'

'Ugh, that certainly is odd. It sounds as though I should have been a bit more cautious with my interviewing and appraisal, but when recent employers give a big tick like the last two did, you reckon that things are okay.'

Nielsen just nodded, gave me a rather weak smile and went next door.

PHILIP

It was another coffee session with Christiane. I enjoy them because it's human company, and very pleasant company at that.

I've had a suspicion after the first time I baked some shortbread that Christiane's more likely to sit down for coffee when shortbread's there, so I've tried to keep up the supply. Not a problem – I'm rather partial to them too. My right arm for stirring the mixture was well enough now, and I'd just got a batch ready.

Anyway, out of the blue Christiane said: 'You know the other day when what I'm sure was Giampaolo chased me up the back lane and you resuscitated me, you played this beautiful record that calmed me down. What was it?'

'It was François Couperin's "Leçons de Ténèbres". It was sung by Alfred Deller.'

'He had a lovely voice, but I haven't heard of him before.'

'He was one of the most famous of countertenors. The music's so gentle, and I just love the rather high but melodious tones of countertenors.

'It's funny but when I was younger I hated sung music that wasn't pop. We used to go to church and hear all those turgid and sanctimonious hymns that Church of England congregations sing – Christian soldiers triumphing over all the heathens and that sort of thing. Also I had an aunt who was keen on lieder and that type of singing. Couldn't stand that either. I believe somebody once said that a tenor singing lieder sounded as though someone had him by the balls and was twisting. I'd agree with that.'

'So what changed?'

'Well, I have to give the credit to France, actually, and the Roman Catholic church. Not that I'm in any way a Catholic.

'My mother died when I was twelve, and my father didn't have much clue about bringing up a son. When I was about sixteen he had this sudden idea that I should learn more French than my school was managing to get into me, and he sent me for two weeks to a language course in the French countryside. It was in an old and rather grand house, on the banks of the River Loire not all that far from Tours.'

'Oh, how lovely! That's where my family moved to when my father first retired from work. I know the area really well, and it's just beautiful.'

'Anyway, the house was run by two elderly ladies who did a sort of good cop/bad cop routine. One was warm and friendly and looked after all the domestic side of the stay, and the other was a total dragon who taught the French with a rod of iron. Almost literally.

'Anyway, on the weekend in the middle of the course we were free to go out for the day, and I went on the Sunday to mass in the Cathedral in Tours, which was Roman Catholic of course. I didn't subscribe to any particular faith by that stage, but a rather nice girl on the language course said she wanted to attend the mass, and she seemed keen to have someone with her. I rather fancied her, and it was a great opportunity to spend a bit more time with her so I went along as well.

'When the service started it was an absolute revelation. I was waiting for more ghastly hymns, but instead that a most delightful, ethereal singing started up, which I think now must have been Gregorian chant. The swell of the beautiful deep voices rose slowly, and it gradually filled the huge cathedral. It reverberated round the whole building, and it was absolutely serene. For the first time in my life I had a sense of what you could call spirituality that connected with me, and it was the music rather than the religion that was the inspiration for it. I think it's a far more appropriate form of worship than Stanford hymns, and I'm sure God thinks so too if he does exist. So it was the French who opened my eyes to this whole new world, and I haven't looked back since.'

'Did you make any progress with the rather nice girl, too?'

'No, I didn't. I was quite keen to and I suggested it, but she went very frosty and said: "I'm not interested in sex". Which wasn't true, because I saw one of the other guys on the course coming out of her bedroom on three separate mornings. What she'd meant, of course, was "I'm not interested in sex with you".'

'Yes, well – you win some and you lose some…'

'I did actually go to bed with one other girl on the course, but it wasn't very exciting. She was ruthlessly bedding every guy on the course in turn, and I didn't like her much anyway. Too much desperation. In my view sex is really only good when it's with someone for whom you have other feelings too.

Just with a stranger for the sake of it doesn't do much for me.'

'I'm certainly not arguing with that.'

'Anyway, that was my education on that course apart from the French language, which I did pick up a certain amount of. You do win some and lose some, but the music was a fabulous reward so I came out well on top.'

'Score one for France there, certainly – très bon. Have you found much more music like that?'

'Yes, quite a bit in fact. It's all in the drawers in the sitting room, under the CD player. Everybody'll have their own preferences, but the things that I've found most beautiful and out of this world are some operatic arias where a solo voice sings something beautiful and gentle, parts of some of the quieter masses, and almost anything sung by certain voices. Those are countertenors among the males, and contraltos and mezzosopranos among the female voices. Especially the contraltos. What I love about those voices is the richness and subtlety of the tones – much more complex than a straight soprano or tenor.

'So if you're interested just dig around in the drawers and play them any time you like. No need to have a trauma first, in fact I'd prefer it if you didn't. My nursing skills probably aren't up to much more than your scratches the other day. If you want to start with one of the best countertenors I've ever heard, I can recommend the disc by Andreas Scholl – I think it's in the top drawer. And among the composers give Gesualdo, Pergolesi and Victoria a go, maybe Lassus and Palestrina as well. And Johannes Ockeghem – he's one of the best, actually. He wrote back in the 1400s, but it's as fresh now as it would have been then. Anyway, I won't bore you by listing them all. Just dig around in the drawers and try them.'

'That sounds great - thank you, and I might just do that.'

And several times later when I was upstairs at the computer I heard more than one of the CDs being played, which pleased me more than anything.

CHRISTIANE

I thought it was about time I did some cooking for the two of us, since Philip wasn't quite up to that yet. He'd cooked a risotto for me the day I moved in, and some personal pride has been telling me that I need to cook a proper dish to establish my cuisine credentials. Cuisine as opposed to food preparation.

I decided that my French heritage demanded a cassoulet, which I thought would be a good, hearty dish to restore an injured patient and take his mind off the still slightly lingering pain.

My mother was a very good cook, and cassoulet was one of the dishes she was most proud of. My father hadn't the slightest interest in cooking – only in eating the results – and my three older brothers were too concerned with playing with their friends to be interested in the kitchen. Then a daughter came along and she must have hoped that I'd turn out like her. She was an attractive woman with a well-rounded figure, full-breasted and feminine. Instead I had a figure almost exactly like my skinny brothers, except in the one regard, and my mother must have wondered what was wrong with her genes that she couldn't even pass them on to me.

I know I was a disappointment to her in many ways, but she persisted at least with the cooking, and I think I turned out a reasonable pupil in the end. And I learned not just cassoulet but quite a few useful recipes, from French cuisine and more widely.

So I felt confident now in trying this, even though I hadn't cooked anything serious for quite a while. I hadn't of course had the opportunity at Mrs Marshall's. I thought very briefly that I might cheat by using tinned beans, but I decided that with my French heritage honour demanded that I must do it the proper way, so I told Philip I'd do it for the next day – I'd find something simple for tonight. Philip already had some dried haricot beans in the cupboard, so I put some of those to soak overnight for the cassoulet.

Next day was a Saturday, so I had plenty of time for cooking. My memories of my mother were coming back and I knew roughly what I was in for, so I went out to buy the remaining ingredients. Only the duck was a bit of a problem. Most butchers wanted advance notice to get one in, but eventually I found one at a small butcher in the Lancaster market. In addition I had a stroke of luck with something that I spotted in a delicatessen in the market, and I was looking forward to introducing Philip to it.

I also owed Philip one for the wine that he'd provided with his risotto, so I looked around for a good and robust French red. That was even harder than the duck, but I found a nice-sounding burgundy at a wine shop also in the market. I just hoped that they'd stored it correctly.

I par-cooked the beans, then set them aside and heated the pork fat. My mother had always used duck fat, but that was asking too much of Lancaster and the book said that pork fat could be used instead. I cooked up each of the meats in turn, then chopped the cooked meat into chunks and started preparing the vegetables. Finally I assembled the whole dish.

I'd read that the traditional way to cook a cassoulet was to bake it for several hours and then let it cool, then do that again and maybe yet once more. With that long cooking it forms a natural crust of condensed ingredients. However, that would have taken far too long, and I know my mother, when she was very busy, cheated occasionally like other cooks have done and put a crust of breadcrumbs on it instead. So I sprinkled breadcrumbs on mine too, and put the whole dish in the oven to bake. To go with it I made a salad of bitter lettuce and a few other well-flavoured ingredients as a contrast to the rich main dish. And as I was doing this all properly, I mixed my own dressing.

Philip stuck his head through the door at one stage.

'If it's as good as it smells now, I might even stay for dinner....'

I put my tongue out at him. 'I'm quite sure it won't be, so you'd better start making other plans.'

He grinned, and I went on with preparing the *bouquet garni*. I was looking forward to telling Philip that it was his rosemary and his thyme in the dish – it sort of made it a more friendly affair. Though actually I do think of them as our herbs these days – I did add a mint plant the other day, as well as the earlier thyme.

This place is actually feeling more like home than I'd expected it would when I moved in. I love my eagle's nest at the top of the house, and the house is quite comfortable in general. And it's nice to have the company of Philip at times, odd though he can be at times – he's never intrusive. It's all far better than my poky room at Mrs Marshall's.

Dinner time approached, and I told Philip he should come down a bit early to have a small amuse-bouche before the meal. When he arrived I gave him a glass of wine, and then served a plate of pieces of cheese on the plainest cracker biscuits that I could find.

'Please try one of these and tell me if you like it or not.'

He looked slightly puzzled, but took one and ate it. And then looked delighted.

'This is absolutely delicious. I've never had a cheese like it before. What on earth is it?'

'I never expected to find it in Lancaster, but I came across it in the small deli near the butcher's when I was buying the other ingredients this morning. It's Ossau Iraty, and it's a sheep's milk cheese from the far south-west of France. The Ossau valley is in Béarn province in the Pyrenees and the Irati Forest is in the Basque country nearby. But why I'm so delighted to have found it and introduced you to it – apart from the fact that it's a lovely cheese – is that it comes from where I was born and grew up for my early years.

'As well as producing delicious cheese the area's known for its wines. We didn't have anything to do directly with either product, but my father was a cooper, I think it's called in English. He made barrels and casks for wines.

'He was a very skilled craftsman, and when I was about seven he was poached by a wine cooperative in the Loire region, and we moved up there. I missed the mountainous wildness of the Pyrenees – you couldn't get anywhere much flatter than the Loire valley. Well, you'd know that from when you went on that French course you were telling me about. It's flat, though I'd have to agree that it's also very beautiful, and it has all those magnificent chateaux.

'Tragically, a couple of years or so into that work my father suffered a serious work accident and he had to stop altogether. He lost his pride as well as his livelihood, and he faded away and died a year later. It was a very hard thing for a youngish child to watch.'

'I know exactly what you mean there,' murmured Philip, but he didn't elaborate.

'We were lucky that my mother was also able to earn a good income. She was a book editor, which was great in that she could be flexible about moving to a new area, and she could also be in her work hours while she was looking after my father. She was a strong and positive woman, and she managed to get us all through the trauma. I've always admired her for that.

'Anyway, my mother who had a good professional reputation then got a very good offer of a book-editing position in London, and we moved over to this country. That's how I came to be somewhat anglicised in the end. Or maybe just a hotch-potch of both.'

'I wouldn't call it a hotch-potch – I think you've got some of the better characteristics of both nations. Let's call it a good cocktail instead. And I'm delighted to have had this cheese to celebrate the mixture.'

'It is nice, isn't it? I love its firmish texture, and I think the taste is exquisite. Even in a nation with as many different cheeses as France has, they prize it highly. I believe it's one of only two sheep's milk cheeses apart from Roquefort that has an AOC status – that's Appellation d'Origine Contrôlée.'

'And I can see how it would deserve that. Thank you so much for sharing this – both the cheese and the memories. You realise, though, that the dinner's going to have to be very good after this...'

I didn't say anything, but I gave him a challenging stare – trying not to grin.

And when we finally ate it the cassoulet was good – even I had to admit that. The wine wasn't bad either – not quite up with the Grand Cru wines from that region, but not too bad.

We cleared our palates at the end with some fresh blueberries – beautifully crisp and sharp.

Philip's praise seemed very genuine, and honour was satisfied. Finally I was feeling a bit more settled again, and Philip seemed more relaxed than he had been for a while, so I thought I'd add to his positive thoughts.

'I'd just like to say that I'm really enjoying living in this house. It has a very nice atmosphere to it.'

'I know what you mean – I like it a lot as well. I think it must be Aunt Clarissa's benign oversight of it. It's not even too much work to look after.'

'I still don't feel that you should do as much of the cleaning as you do – do feel free to get me to share it.'

'I really don't find it as tedious as things like the ironing. I'm certainly not a fan of that.'

'Well if you don't mind me saying, you could save yourself a significant amount of effort if you didn't iron your bedsheets.'

He looked a bit startled at that. 'Doesn't everyone iron sheets?'

'In our grandmothers' day maybe, but even my mother didn't do hers and I certainly don't. Yes with pillowcases and duvet covers, but not with base sheets.'

'Well, I'm glad you told me – I just wish you'd been around years ago! My problem is that not having had a mother around at the critical times, I've just had to guess how all these things are done. And I obviously got that one wrong.'

I don't think I offended him – in fact I think he was pleased at the thought of saving a chore. Then we started chatting about creativity – I can't remember now what got us on to that subject. Philip said: 'I don't have a creative bone in my body. I love listening to music, but I can't play anything and I can't sing, and I can't draw or paint. How about you – are you expert on anything?'

'Not really, but when I was younger I loved art. We had a great teacher at my school who both taught and encouraged us, and I always thought I did quite well. I liked watercolours the best – less garish than typical oil paintings unless they're done by the masters. I loved the delicacy. But circumstances haven't been right in recent years and I haven't done any for a while.'

'Do you have any here that I could have a look at?' he asked, rather cautiously.

'No, I'm sorry but my mother has them all in London. She rather liked them, and I had nowhere to store them. You saw my previous room in Mrs Marshall's house.'

'Yes, point taken. But there's stacks of room here, including in the cellar which is well lit. You'd be most welcome to take it up again if you'd like. Unless you're thinking of leaving soon, of course?'

He sounded a bit wistful as he said the last bit.

'Thanks very much for that offer, and I'll certainly think about it. Unless you're thinking of throwing me out any time soon, of course?'

His grin looked a bit like relief.

'Well, I have been thinking about it, of course, but I've decided to do nothing about it for the moment….'

He should have looked a bit more serious as he said that.

* * *

I lay in bed later thinking of Philip on that earlier occasion when he'd started talking about choral music. The subject was interesting, but what was far more remarkable was the sudden and enormous animation that he showed as he spoke about it. I don't think I've ever seen him look so excited about anything since I've been in the flat. In fact I don't think I've ever seen him react to anything much, except maybe in a small way on the idea of visiting Thai hill tribes. However, on the subject of choral music he really came alive. A sign of a human being in there after all.

I may have been a bit wrong in some of my other judgements too, because although he is a wimp in some ways he wasn't slow in facing up to Giampaolo's attempts at bullying. OK, he didn't come off best in the encounter, but that wasn't totally his fault. The hallway step was fighting for Giampaolo's team, unfortunately. I have to give him marks for his effort there too. I just can't work out why he spends so much of his time apparently tucked away in some sort of shell. I need to find some way to crack the shell open, and persuade him to be fully human.

PHILIP

I was getting used to knocks on the door, but I still twitched slightly. However, it was only the friendly face of Sergeant Nielsen again. He came in and sat in the front room, where Christiane was also sitting.

'We haven't apprehended your attacker yet, sir, but we've had reports that he's now in London. I'm guessing that he'll stay clear of this area for a while, so you should be able to live without any worry. Both of you...' he added with a look at Christiane. 'And if he does come back and causes either of you any more trouble, just give me a quick bell. He's down in the books now, and we'll be straight down on him, hard.'

Christiane looked at me as he said that, but I wasn't going to say anything.

'Thank God – that's great news. No developments on the other front, I suppose?'

'That's the other matter I came to see you about, actually. We've now had a very thorough look around Ms Mason's house, and there's absolutely nothing that would give us any clue as to what might have happened, or whether there's anything unusual or suspect in her background. Normally we'd just give up and try other lines of enquiry at this stage, but there aren't too many other lines of enquiry we can follow. I just have a gut feeling that we ought to be able to see something in the house. Something about all this isn't adding up, but I can't put my finger on what it is.'

He paused, and then said: 'I wondered whether you might be prepared to come and have a look yourself with us? You're the only person we can find at the moment who's had any recent contact with her, and something might just strike you that we haven't seen.'

'I'd certainly be prepared to do that – I'm as keen as you are to see the culprit found for this.'

After a bit of discussion we agreed on the following afternoon, meeting at Rosemary's house.

* * *

At the due time at the house I found Sergeant Nielsen and a young male constable.

'This is PC Garfield who helped with the earlier search of this house. I thought it might be handy in case you have any queries about what he might already have done in here. Feel free to look around the whole house. If you want to open any cupboards or drawers you can do so, but please only carefully or ask me to be with you. We've made a very thorough search and finger-printed it already, so you wouldn't be compromising any evidence.'

I have to admit that my imagination was floundering at the

thought of what they were hoping me to do. I've never searched anyone's house before, let alone someone who's been involved in a major crime. I could only hope that my prior – if brief – experience with Rosemary Mason might let me see something that the others wouldn't.

Which hope was soon dashed. The house was pretty unexceptional. It was neat and tidy – perhaps remarkably so, but I know that some people are very fastidious about that sort of thing. It seemed to have everything that a house should have, and nothing at all out of the ordinary.

The furniture was simple – quite comfortable by the look of it. It was all pretty much of the same age and style – rather like a job lot that someone might have bought to furnish a motel or something like that.

The bookshelf was not full, but had a fair number of books in it – mostly recent fiction as far as I could see. No crime books that I noticed – more light general fiction, perhaps with a slight tendency towards romance though not really Mills and Boon.

The larder had a basic stock of supplies, all quite normal for any kitchen. The ironing basket was empty.

The upstairs rooms were equally unremarkable. The bathroom was neat and clean, with no unusual items in it – toothpaste and brush, hairbrush, and the sort of pharmaceuticals and makeup products that would be found in any woman's house. Normal amounts of all of them. The bedrooms were tidy and looked comfortable without being lavish. One novel by Joanna Trollope was on what was presumably Rosemary's bedside table, and there was nothing much else apart from a nice-looking clock, probably moderately old. That was almost the only thing in the house that wasn't completely ordinary.

I had to admit defeat to Nielsen and Garfield.

'Absolutely nothing is jumping out at me. I haven't of course been through all the drawers in detail – did you see anything there that seemed at all unusual?'

Nielsen looked at Garfield, who said:

'I did most of that searching, Sarge, and I didn't really find a thing. Pots and pans, cutlery, mats, clothing – all the usual stuff for any house. There was only one drawer that had papers in it, and they were mostly bills, bank statements and things like that. There was a birth certificate, in the name of Rosemary Mason. No passport, but that's not unusual. No driving licence either – that's a bit more surprising, though she doesn't seem to have had a car at least at the moment. Not really anything else, either.'

Nielsen said: 'Oh well, it was worth a try. I wasn't hugely optimistic but we have to try everything.'

And we went our different ways.

A PERSON AS YET UNNAMED

There's been quite a lot in the papers about the woman who was found on the railway line – more of a hoo-hah than I was expecting. A bit of a bugger that she was pulled off the line before a train went over her, so the police now know she was strangled. I hadn't reckoned on that.

I'd been very careful, though, and I don't think there's any way they're going to connect her with me. Her real identity's made it safe so far because the police haven't worked out who she was. Let's hope it stays that way.

I thought back to the night when it all happened. That bloody bitch had well and truly asked for it. I thought she wasn't going to appear, until the door opened quietly and she slipped in.

I said: 'You're late. I thought you weren't coming.'

'Well, I have come, but this is the last time. I've got to move on in my life.'

'What do you mean, the last time? I can tell people who you were and what you've been doing, and you won't get any peace then.'

'Well, that works two ways. I'll tell people what you've been doing to patients, and you won't get much peace then either. In whichever jail you're in.'

'You bitch, you can't do that.' I went to grab her, and the bloody woman had the hide to pull a knife on me. A small but sharp looking peeling knife or something.

I dodged the knife and grabbed her round the throat and squeezed as hard as I could. She struggled hard at first, and then I saw her eyes bulging, her face redden, and her mouth gaping with her tongue beginning to stick out. Then she went limp and I realised after a moment that I'd probably killed her.

The bitch, the bloody bitch. I hadn't wanted her dead, but it was all her fault. She should never have pulled a knife on me.

I looked at her body, and noticed that in the struggle the knife had cut one of her arms quite badly. There was blood on her sleeve, and on the blanket of the bed on which I'd put her. Too bad. I know how to dispose of the clothes, and nobody ever comes into this room to see the blood there. At least I didn't seem to have any of it on me.

I stopped then and thought about what I'd done. Her bloody fault – she should never have threatened me. But what to do now?

Well, I did think of one thing, which would bloody well serve her right. I checked my watch. Plenty of time. Never done a dead body before. There's a first time for anything. Use a condom – no evidence of me if the body's found later.

The slut. The bloody slut. She'd asked for it – it was all her fault.

* * *

After the pleasure I realised I had to think a bit more clearly. I had a body, and I had to do something with it – quick, before all the morning movements were going to start.

I thought of carting it out to Lancaster Moor or somewhere like that – nice and remote with no pointers to anyone. But there wasn't going to be time for that. Just hiding it somewhere here was no option either – nowhere would have been private enough to be sure that it wasn't found. Then I thought of the railway cutting. It's almost level with one edge of the hospital grounds, but it's regularly used by people at night for sex on the railway bank so the police would think it was that. And I reckon if the police don't know who she really is, they won't make any links to here.

It wasn't a very large body, so I humped her over my shoulder and took her to my car which was just out the back. Ten minutes' drive to the bridge over the railway, and I heaved her down and along the track a bit. Luckily the shaggers had all gone by then.

I laid her down with her neck across the railway line, so the next train would run over her and get rid of the marks round her neck. That was to make things even harder for the police.

I was only away for forty minutes in all, and everything was still quiet when I got back. Nobody'd stirred at that time of night – no problem. I put her clothes in one of my drawers – I'll get rid of them soon where nobody'll ever find them.

PHILIP

Lying in bed that night I couldn't sleep – I kept seeing Rosemary Mason's house, and thinking that if only I'd had a bit more imagination I might have spotted something.

And then an idea crossed my mind. Women can think differently from men, and as far as I knew the house had been searched by men like Nielsen and Garfield. Maybe a WPC would see something else – or maybe even Christiane if she'd be prepared to do it. I know that she has a good and imaginative mind, and I think a good understanding of people.

In the morning we coincided for breakfast, and I put the idea to her. She was initially rather hesitant, but in the end she agreed as long as it was OK with the police.

She said: 'I'd be doing it for Rosemary Mason's sake. I'd really like to see whoever did that to her caught.'

Later I phoned Sergeant Nielsen and put the idea to him. There was a distinct pause and I thought he was going to veto the idea, but then he said:

'That would be all right by me. None of it's proper procedure anyway, but we're really stuck at the moment and I understand what you're saying about a woman's viewpoint. I don't think in fact we did have any WPCs in on this search, which was a mistake on our part because we're supposed to use them when the subject's a female. Would you like to ask Ms Guchez?'

'I have already. She's right here, so would you like to nominate a time?'

After a bit of negotiation we settled for late that afternoon.

When we went to Rosemary Mason's house, Sergeant Nielsen was there but nobody else. I wondered whether that was because he wasn't really supposed to be having both of us there, but that was his decision. He repeated the same cautions as on the previous day.

The three of us wandered round the house, appraising it generally and on occasion poking a bit further.

Silence reigned, and although I tried to wipe my mind clean I still couldn't find anything to comment on. The house was so featureless – not a clue in sight.

But the lack of features might in fact have been the clue, because after a while Christiane said:

'There's something wrong with this house. In a normal house you'd get a variety of furniture of different ages and styles because they've been acquired at different times or by different members of the family. This lot looks as though someone got hold of a furniture store catalogue and ordered two lounge chairs, a sofa, a dining table with four chairs and so on. It's all exactly the same age and style.

'The whole place is also completely devoid of anything personal. Not a single photo, family souvenir, anything that might give others an indication of who the person was. I know some don't hoard as much as others, but I refuse to believe that anyone has absolutely nothing personal around their house. I don't know if she rented this place or owned it, but even rented there'd have been something.'

Nielsen and I stood in silence digesting the thought, until Christiane added: 'I get a strong feeling that Rosemary Mason was trying to hide her true identity. And I speak as someone who's had to do that in the past as well.'

Further silence, then Sergeant Nielsen said: 'You might just be right there. I think that's why I said earlier that there was something wrong about the place, but I just couldn't put my finger on what it was. That's a great help, because there's several ways in which we can now try to find out why an identity may have been hidden. One of them, of course, could be by the law itself, if she was a protected witness or something.'

He grinned at Christiane. 'Well done – I knew it would be a good move to ignore regulations for once.' He turned to me and winked again. 'Just don't tell Inspector Brady, will you.'

PHILIP

When we got home I thought we needed something a bit special for dinner again, so I suggested that I cook Chinese. I like it but there's no point in doing it for one person – not much more for two, I'd agree, but it's at least possible.

I asked Christiane, and after looking doubtful for a moment she accepted. So I thawed some meat from the freezer, and I cooked beef in oyster sauce with broccoli and water chestnuts, and Kung Po chicken. They were both recipes that Lucy had taught me. Long grain rice with both, and two mangos that I'd just bought to follow. I was quite proud of the selection.

Christiane went out to get a bottle of white wine from the off-licence, while I set the table with Chinese bowls and chop-sticks – no European cutlery.

She returned with the wine. I laid out the dishes, and with an exaggerated wave of my arm I said: "*S'il vous plait, madame…*". Then on a sudden impulse I said: "Or am I now allowed to say *s'il te plait*?".

She gave me a longish look, then grinned and said: "*Je t'en prie, Philippe…*".

I particularly liked the Philippe. Much more style than Philip.

We sat down, and I was a bit surprised when Christiane looked a bit dubious and said she'd never eaten with chopsticks before. She can't have had any Asian guys amongst her string of admirers.

'Well, this is a great chance to learn then. Quite easy, and it's the only way to eat Chinese, morsel by morsel instead of all heaped together in a spoon when you don't get the subtlety and the flavours. Pick up your chopsticks like this.' I showed her how to lay one across the centre of her hand, and the other above it, coming down on it to secure the food.

'See how you can waggle one up and down to snag the food – practise it for a moment while I get the dishes out.'

After a few false starts she got the hang quite well, and by the end of the meal she wasn't bad. Which she didn't fail to comment on, but she'd earned it.

She said: 'I guess you learned this from your girlfriend Lucy?'

'Yes, she was a good cook and keen to teach people about Chinese food. She had three main loves in life – making money, cooking and sex. Probably in that order, though making money was a long way ahead of the other two. I'm guessing that you never had any Asians among all your boyfriends at university?'

She gave me a rather funny look. 'You sound as though you think I was a loose woman there?'

Oops, minefield looming. 'I thought that you had an active love life, and I have to say I think that's all good. It made you the person you are, which is definitely a compliment. I only wish I could claim the same – I'd have been a better person for it, too.'

Minefield skirted – I think. Anyway, the meal appeared to go down all right, chopsticks and all.

As we relaxed with the meal and the wine, Christiane asked: 'Does anyone ever call you Phil instead of Philip?'

'Not really, which is fine by me because I hate it. Philip isn't a particularly distinguished name anyway, but it's better than Phil.' Then I added: 'And I'd have to say that Philippe was the nicest of all!'

I thought for a moment. 'Does anyone ever call you Chris? I don't think I ever heard that at uni.'

'Thank God no – I hate it too. I get called various things because my name's unusual for the English, but I can't stand Chris. I get Christine quite often, from people who think my name's been misspelled. And our really nice pest control officer who comes to the department always calls me Christina. I've put him right a few times, but it doesn't stick and I actually quite like Christina. At least from him – he's a lovely guy.'

'So did your family always call you Christiane?'

'In the rather contrary way of families they actually called me Annie, but that was a strictly family nickname. I quite like it, but I haven't been called that for years. But I like Christiane best of all because it reminds me of a very brave and smart lady – Christiane Amanpour.'

'Who's she? I don't think I've heard the name.'

'She's a very senior international journalist, for both CNN and ABC. I admire her because she's spoken out when she's felt that she had to, even though at times it's been controversial. She believes that a reporter can't be absolutely neutral and do their job effectively, and I'm inclined to believe that. She's also prepared to go to some pretty dangerous places, which I admire. If you play safe all the time you don't achieve anything. I can't claim to share any of her virtues, but I'm happy to share the nice name with her.'

'She does indeed sound like quite a lady. Thank God there are some like that around.'

She might think she doesn't share any of those characteristics, but I think she has elements of some. It says a few things about Christiane's approach to life.

And maybe I should find out a bit more about Christiane Amanpour – she sounds interesting.

LANCASTER POLICE HQ

Inspector Brady was actually looking cheerful for once. The station's computer whiz had been searching databases for why Rosemary Mason might have had her name protected, and she'd found her. It wasn't witness protection, however. Rosemary Mason was the new name for Rhonda Miller, who killed her husband with a kitchen knife after several years of very violent domestic abuse. She was tried for murder, and acquitted on the grounds that it was justified self-defence. The trial received national press publicity, and the public was strongly divided on the verdict with both sides holding their opinions vehemently.

Given those feelings she would never have been able to return safely to an open community, so she was given a new name and a carefully guarded identity like a protected witness. There was one other unusual feature which was that she had had to undergo a short spell in a mental hospital, partly to settle her back to a life without domestic abuse but partly also to assess that she would genuinely be no risk to the community if and when she was released.

Inspector Brady called his team together, and they discussed the implications of this new information.

Brady said: 'You'll probably all remember Ms Mason's trial. It made the national headlines for days, not only because of the verdict which quite a few people disagreed with, but because a number of pretty nasty characters spoke out publicly and said they'd make sure that proper justice was done. I reckon we should go after all of them straight away and see where we get to. We can't one hundred per cent discount things like Mason being killed by somebody she'd been having random sex with by the railway, or a random attack by someone who didn't even know her, but I'd put my money on one of the low-lifes from the trial first off. Any thoughts from the rest of you?'

Sergeant Nielsen was first to speak. 'Sir, that would fit better with the timeline – her being killed a couple of hours before the body was dropped off at the railway. She could have been grabbed by one of the people who made the threats – maybe kept for a bit while they told her what was going to happen to her and why. I don't think there were any signs of torture, though, were there?'

'I don't recall any from the post mortem report, no.'

'Well, once he'd done it he'd be faced with getting rid of the body. It might have taken him a while to work out how and where. Or maybe he was just waiting until it was really quiet in the small hours.'

'Thanks, Len – I think we're singing from the same song-sheet. Anyone else?'

Rather tentatively, PC Hobbs said: 'Why would she have been placed like she was on the railway, with her neck over the line like that?'

'Fair question. Maybe he was just being vindictive – wanting her to be mutilated – head chopped off or something. I don't know, but I don't think it rules out one of the people from the trial. Anyone else got anything to add?'

PC Garfield spoke up. 'What about the knife wounds on her right arm, sir? The pathologist reckoned they were recent, about the same time as the strangulation. But if she was strangled, why knife cuts as well?'

'Mm, fair question too. Maybe he was torturing her before-hand after all. We'll have to keep as open a mind as we can on this. Any more from anyone?'

There was the usual slight shuffling, but otherwise silence.

'Right then, we know what's got to be done next. Len – will you organise a thorough search of trial records and then get a team together to chase all of them up for alibis.'

'I'll get on to it straight away, sir. The rest of you – don't leave town – you'll have some work to do.'

SERGEANT NIELSEN

I knew I was going to cop this job – following up on all the people who made threats or comments against Rosemary Mason, or Rhonda Miller as she still was at her trial, when she was acquitted of murdering her husband. Well, I suppose it's better than being pensioned off. Maybe.

I sent young Jimmy Garfield round to the newspaper office to see if their reporting had any of the names in it, and I dug out our files on the case and the trial and settled down with a cup of strong coffee to try and work up a bit of stamina.

* * *

Jimmy was at the paper office for a couple of hours, and he came back looking quite pleased with himself.

'I got eleven names from the old newspaper reports, Sarge. I reckon that's not a bad haul.'

'Aye, well yer not done yet. You've got to find out where they all are now so we can interview them. Get to it.'

His face fell, and I hadn't meant to be quite so sharp.

'You did well, lad. You know that if you nail the bastard you get a bonus?'

'Oh aye?' He didn't sound convinced.

'Yeah, I buy you a pint at the Crown and Feathers….'

His expression said it all.

* * *

My work on the reports wasn't helped by a series of petty crimes I had to attend to, and it was a couple of days before I'd got through the records properly. Some at least of the people were probably just bigots who'd shot off a comment and that was the end of it. We'd have to chase them all up, but there were six who did stand out from the rest.

The first was a Frank Higginbotham. He'd attended every day of Rosemary Mason's trial. When she was found not guilty of murder he yelled out in court that justice was not being done, and he gave an interview to the press afterwards outside the court building. He wouldn't listen to the reporters who said that the husband had beaten Rosemary up regularly, and he seemed to be one of those who think that a husband has the right to do anything they like to a wife. It'd be worth looking him up to see if he has any record for assaulting a wife, or anyone else, and then going to interview him about this case.

The second name that came up was a bit more sinister. Dermot O'Leary had also been at Rosemary Mason's trial, though he didn't create any sort of disturbance. However, he was noted to have been staring very intently at her during the proceedings, and he had a record of stalking and harassing single women. He was waiting outside the court when the trial finished, apparently peering around for Mason, but she of course was taken away in custody to be admitted to the Royal Victoria Hospital so he failed there. But he could have seen her later and started pestering her, and she might have been reluctant to report it after her previous run in with the law.

The third was Rosemary Mason's brother-in-law, Harley Miller, who never accepted that his brother – Rosemary's husband – had been a violent man, and he swore after the trial that he'd see that justice – as he saw it – was done. Given the blood relationship with the murdered man, he'd be well worth close questioning.

The fourth was Albert Jones, who had several previous convictions for domestic violence, and there was currently a restraining order out against him in relation to his wife. Who was trying hard to become his ex-wife. He was noted as muttering a lot during the trial, and he had to be warned by the judge at one stage, at which point he stormed out of the court calling out that the trial was a farce. He also had a number of convictions for public drunkenness, sometimes involving general violence.

The fifth was Raymond Ackerley. He also had a record of convictions, for producing and distributing pornography. It was well known that he regarded women as sexual objects created for men's pleasure. He was noted as attending every day of the trial, and making copious notes for much of it. He also stared very intently at the accused for a lot of the time, and the police reporter noted that he regarded Ackerley's general demeanour and behaviour as concerning.

The last on our list was the founder of a supposed "movement for men's rights". Eberhard Schulz was the founder of something he called the "Men's Justice Movement", which was dedicated to giving men back the rights that they used to have before the plague of women's liberation. This included men having sole control over the family finances, women being at the beck and call of the master whenever he chose, and a man's right to discipline his wife if she did undesirable things. One could only guess what that might include. He was known in his district as the "nasty nutty Nazi", but it was by no means clear that he was nutty. Though nasty, certainly.

It was not clear whether the "Men's Justice Movement" had any members other than Eberhard Schulz, but he'd set it up with letterhead, signs, etc., as though it was a proper organisation. He liked to play the role of a pompous father-figure, with overtones of a preacher, and he also called out when the verdict was announced that the Lord would deliver true justice in due time.

All in all they were a charming bunch, and I'm really looking forward to interviewing them all. Or not. I'll need to set up a good cop-bad cop pairing, so I picked PC Brian Hawkins, who has an angelic face at any time (though only the face). He can be the good cop, and he can take the lead in the questioning. I'll do the bad cop as necessary, and if I can't come over as tough enough I'm sure I can get Inspector Brady in to do some real heavying. He's good at that.

PHILIP

We had yet another visit a few days later from Sergeant Nielsen. Luckily Christiane was here at the time, because I think he was beginning to be another of her keen admirers.

'You were spot on with your comment on concealed identities. We managed to get access to a very secure database, and we found that she did have official help to change her identity.

'It wasn't witness protection, though. You might or might not remember a case in west Yorkshire about five years ago where a woman stabbed her husband to death. He was a truly cruel and abusive man' – he paused to look at Christiane at that point – 'and the trial found that she was literally in fear of her life when she did it. Justifiable homicide. But there was an enormous public hoo-ha after the verdict – a lot praised her for standing up to violence, but some – all men, if I remember right – were practically clamouring for public hanging to be brought back.

'As a result the authorities decided that she should be given a new identity because her life would still have been under threat if she hadn't. I can only tell you all this now because she's dead.

'But the reason why these facts coming to light is so important is that the trial judge considered that Rosemary Mason, as she became, had at least suffered a temporary mental problem, and he recommended a spell in a mental hospital. And guess which hospital – none other than the Royal Victoria Hospital in Lancaster. That immediately gives us a local connection that might be relevant.

'The Royal Victoria was a slightly unusual choice, because it's more of a home for those who used to be called "simple". Psychiatric cases normally go to Lancaster Moor Hospital. However, as far as we can determine the authorities considered that although she was technically regarded as a psychiatric case she wasn't a danger to anyone any longer, and they didn't want to put her among other potentially violent patients. I guess they felt she'd had her fill of violence.

'She was discharged from the hospital nearly four years ago – her treatment didn't take long. We're currently trying to find out a bit more about her time in the hospital in case there's a connection with what's happened now, but we're having some trouble getting anywhere. Not so much official secrecy this time, more that the hospital records don't seem to be as well organised as they ought to be.

'The other line that we're following up is people who came out at the time and said that she should be hanged or whatever. If there's someone who felt strongly and was a bit unhinged, he could have made it his obsession to track her down and hurt her in some way. We'll have trouble because there won't be records of all the people who spoke out, but we can see what we might be able to find.'

'It's very kind of you to tell us all this. Much appreciated.'

Nielsen looked at Christiane and smiled rather grimly. 'It's Miss Guchez who earned this. If you hadn't said what you said the other day we probably wouldn't be here now.'

Christiane said: 'I weep for the poor woman – saved from one awful fate only to find another. I just hope you can get somewhere now.'

SERGEANT NIELSEN

Young Jimmy Garfield surprised me. I'd told him I'd investigate the six main suspects who'd threatened Rosemary Mason, but in five days he'd chased down quite a few of the other eleven names that he'd got from the newspaper reports, plus several extras from our files on the trial.

That was the good news, but the less good was that not many of them could be in the frame for the killing. One was confirmed to have died, and another was senile and bedridden. A third had emigrated to New Zealand, and a fourth was living in South Devon. While he could just have come back to Lancaster to commit the deed, there was no evidence that he did. Yet another was local, but it seemed likely that he would have been incapably drunk at the time of night when Rosemary Mason was killed – something that was confirmed by his wife who said he was paralytic every night. And none of the others was likely either.

For the rest the hunt still went on.

I'd decided that I should follow up first on Harley Miller,

the brother of Rosemary Mason's husband, so I called him to get him in for an interview. He wasn't keen, but when I said we could do it by calling in at his workplace – in force – he decided that maybe our interview room was the best.

He was a nasty and truculent character. I hadn't met him when the trial was on, but the notes in the file weren't too flattering about him.

'You'll have read in the papers that your brother's ex was found strangled the other day. We're looking at all the people who'd made negative comments about her at the time of her trial.'

'I didn't hear anything about that, and I read the papers well enough.'

'She'd had her name changed to Rosemary Mason after the acquittal.'

'Oh aye? Well nobody ever told me that. Yes, I do remember reading something about that in the papers, and it weren't before time if you ask me. The bitch. I'd have done it meself only I didn't.'

'So where were you in the evening of Saturday the tenth of June?'

'Buggered if I know, but me usual thing of a Saturday night's to go to the pub for a few hours and then home to the missus. She'll confirm that.'

I didn't have any proof that he might have been in the relevant area, but we went back to his home just to check. It turned out that his wife had gone that weekend to stay with her sister in Wigan, so she couldn't confirm anything. Miller maintained that he'd been at the pub anyway, and in the absence at the moment of any evidence of his possible involvement I had to leave it. It's possible that the pub might have CCTV which would show whether he'd been there that night. If they'd still got the tape, that is, and not all pubs have the cameras anyway.

I thought of one more thing to ask before I left. He'd driven back from the station to his home in a light grey Vauxhall sedan, but he could have a second car of course.

'Do you by any chance own a white estate car?'

He glared at me. 'You saw the car I was driving. We're not made of money like some people, you know. That's it.'

He wasn't all that likely, and he could have been lying when he said that he didn't know about the change of identity. Harley Miller wasn't completely out of the frame yet.

PHILIP

Back at home I kept thinking about this new information on the change of identity. There seemed to be at least a chance that there was some sort of connection with the Royal Victoria Hospital, and I wondered if we could find out a bit more about what goes on inside there. Time to use a possible lead in.

'Christiane – you know you've got that pest control officer who does your computer rooms. Didn't you say that he's the pest control officer for the Royal Victoria Hospital as well?'

'Yes – that's his main job. Why?'

'Well, Sergeant Nielsen said he thought that Rosemary Mason had some connection with the hospital. I just thought that your guy might know a bit about it from the other side.'

Silence for a moment while she thought about it, then: 'I suppose it couldn't hurt. I'll ask him if we could come in to see him some time.'

It took a couple of days, but she came back with: 'Frank Elliott said he'd be happy for us to come and visit him at the hospital. I think he likes to have visitors in his little domain.' She grinned. 'I think he wants to see what you're like too! He's my honorary uncle, sort of.'

Oh Gawd…

The day came for the visit, and I was a bit nervous about what we were in for. Not only from the inhabitants.

We parked as near as we could to the Reception office, but not near enough to avoid some of the local residents. The moment the car stopped there was a man looking in through the side window at me, with a mad grin. Then he pulled the door open and with the most exaggerated flourish of his arm he ushered me out of the car. 'Welcome to me home!', he said loudly.

As we got out of the car we heard barking noises coming from behind a nearby tree. Not a dog barking – a human imitating a dog. Not well. A head then peered round the tree, and a little man with a huge grin came out. He roared with laughter and said 'Bet you thought that were a dog! Wahahaha…' And he raced away over the lawn, still chortling.

On the lawn in the other direction, another man stood in front of a thrush. The thrush was busy digging up worms. The man was swearing loudly at it, hurling great verbal abuse, but doing nothing to chase it. The thrush sensibly continued its digging, and both of them ignored us.

I did wonder then what we were heading into, but Frank had assured Christiane that we'd be okay.

Reception was at the top of a magnificent stone stairway, which had broad steps with a low wall on either side that came down in a widening sweep from the top. Behind it the hospital buildings rose and spread out in massive rectangularity. The style was extreme Victorian Gothic, with elaborate ornamentation that reminded me of pictures of the fairy tale castles along the Rhine. The main building windows were like Gothic windows in a church. The roof areas were of very steep slate, set with large numbers of steeply pointed dormer windows, each with little pointed decorations at the apex. The structure was of enormously thick stone, almost looking buttressed in places, and the crowning glory – or horror depending on your opinion of it – was a central tower, with a tall sloping roof set with five dormer windows at various levels. Across its top was a band of ornamental metalwork, and two small objects like flagpoles stood up from the two ends.

The whole building was of the same artistic period and merit as the late and slightly lamented hallstand of Aunt Clarissa's. On this huge scale it was so awful that it almost became impressive. I wouldn't have liked to call it home, though.

We waited outside the Reception window while they called Frank. A tall, elderly, stooping man was pacing up and down the corridor, hands clasped behind his back, looking agitated and staring intently at the floor. But he paid no attention at all to us. Frank had told Christiane that the patients would be no problem, but he was more used to them than we were.

Frank appeared and gave Christiane a broad grin and a big hug. He was tall and broad-shouldered, slightly weatherbeaten, and he seemed a warm and nice man.

'Hullo Christina. How are yer, lass?' Then he looked at me. 'You must be Philip – how do.' He didn't look very impressed, but nothing new there.

'Anyway, come down to my office and we can have a bit of a yarn.'

We set off along the corridor from Reception, and turned along more corridors, through doors, down staircases, up other stairs – I'd have had no hope of finding my way back again. All along the way Frank was greeting patients or being greeted by them. One elderly lady came up and tried to give him a baseball cap that she'd just been given, but he told her it suited her better than him. He put it on her head and she went off highly delighted. Another man came up and shyly showed Frank his model train, which we all duly admired. I couldn't believe that all the patients would be like this, but I was beginning to see why Frank said we wouldn't have too much trouble.

Frank's office had a chair, and a desk with a row of manuals on it. There was also a broad sink and draining board with sprayers, bottles and packets of chemicals, rubber gloves and other spray paraphernalia. Frank ushered us in and locked the door.

'Don't worry – the locks aren't to keep us safe from the patients – they're to keep the patients from getting at the chemicals. They specially like the rat bait if they can get hold of it. Looks like sweeties. It's a nightmare when I have to put it out – I have to find places where even the keenest patient won't look 'em out, and some of them are pretty keen. Fortunately the rats are still able to find them no matter where I put 'em. Rats are very smart, though half the time they're also smart enough not to eat 'em when they do find 'em. Anyway, tell me what you're interested to find out?'

I looked at Christiane, who nodded back at me so I started.

'I work at the university, but in a different area to Christiane. Quite some weeks ago I interviewed someone called Rosemary Mason for a job, and we offered it to her but she never accepted or turned up to start. A little while later we heard of a female body that was found on the railway tracks near here, but you'd know all about that.'

He nodded.

'Anyway, by chance we found out that my Rosemary was the same person, but she seems to have lived a very quiet life and nobody knows much about her, and the police have been asking me lots of questions about her because I seem to be the only person who'd had any recent contact with her. Then the police discovered that she'd spent a bit of time in this hospital – as a patient – but they haven't had enough to go on to start formal enquiries. I'm appalled by the whole affair, and I'd like the person responsible to be caught.'

'Aye, it were a very nasty business – I remember it. I don't know what I can tell you, though. I don't know the names of most of the patients, and the name you said doesn't mean anything to me.' He thought for a moment. 'But I know someone who might be able to help – Aggie Ransome.'

'Is she one of the staff here?'

Frank laughed. 'Nay. She knows a lot more about what goes on here than most of the staff, though. She's a patient and she's been here just about all of her life. And she never should have been. It still fills me with horror when I think of it. She were a young lassie and she were interfered with by her dirty old uncle. But when he were caught it were all her fault. She were declared to be morally defective and she were put in a home. This home. There was nothing wrong with her mind – never has been, though living here for nigh on sixty-five years does make you a bit peculiar.'

'Are we allowed to meet her?' asked Christiane.

'I don't know about allowed, but there don't seem to be too

many rules around here. I can go and talk to her any time, and if I have a couple of other people in tow, who's to care? She's spent her whole life doing odd jobs around the home – mebbe it gives her a feeling that at least she's some use to someone. She cleans up, she moves things around when they need it, all sorts of things. She wanders round all the wards, and they hardly notice that she's even there, but I think she feels she's part of it and it means that she knows a lot of the people past and present who've been here. I don't rightly know where she'd be at this hour, but Bassingthwaite Lower might be a good place to start. She does spend some time in there. They've got one of them companion dogs there, and she does like to go in and give it a pat at times. Let's go for a bit of a walk.'

We strode through more corridors and down some stairs – not the same as before, as far as I could remember – and more patients greeted Frank. We passed a large auditorium in which an elderly man was lining up rows of chairs.

'Eh oop, Billy – yer last one's not quite straight!'

Billy looked at him and tutted, and made an infinitesimal change to the position.

'It looked pretty straight to me, but he wouldn't have anything to do if he thought it were exactly right. He spends all his days lining the chairs up, mekkin' the tiniest changes back and forth. And the next concert's not for another eight days.'

At that moment a patient passed, pulling along a fair-sized toy sheep on wheels. Frank said: "Eh, I like yer sheep, Michael, but what happened to yer monkey?'

''E's back in the ward in me bed.'

'Oh, that's all right then.'

''ere, Mr Elliott, are yer on tomorrer?'

'Aye, Michael, I'm on tomorrer.'

As we walked on I had to ask: 'Do you have to work on Saturdays, then?'

'Nay, I don't, but if I'd told Michael that I weren't here he'd have had a panic. He just likes to be reassured that he won't be left alone. I think he must have had a bad experience when he were little.'

A bit further on we passed a closed door bearing a notice that read: "Please keep this door locked at all times. Remember what happened to Norman's dinner – it could be yours next time." My mind boggled at that one, but I wasn't game to ask Frank.

Aggie wasn't at Bassingthwaite Lower, but the charge nurse said she might have gone to Tudor. Tudor hadn't seen her, but thought at this hour she was probably at Elmdean, but that wasn't right either. However, on our way out of Elmdean we bumped into her coming our way.

'Eh oop, Aggie, I've brought some mates to meet yer.'

Aggie said nothing, but looked at us rather suspiciously.

'They was wondering if yer ever knew a Rosemary Mason here?'

It was obvious from Aggie's face that she did know the name.

'Dirty, dirty man,' she muttered.

'Who would that be?' asked Frank, but she wouldn't be drawn. She shuffled off muttering: 'Dirty man, dirty man...' and we got no further.

Frank pondered for a moment, then said: 'We might just go back to my office for a moment.'

On the way back we saw another patient who was walking

along bent double. Frank said: 'That lad's a really sad case. He lived on a really isolated farm on t'moors, and his parents kept him in their chicken run. It had a very low roof and he couldn't ever stand up, and he's been bent like that ever since. He can't speak a word, neither. Maybe he can cackle, I don't know, but I've never heard him say a word. It fills me with horror every time I see him – how any parents could treat their child like that. I don't know what happened to 'em when he were found, but they should have been locked up in here as well. Or in the Lancaster Moor hospital.'

I couldn't say anything – I was dumbstruck by the horror of his condition. He was so bent it must have been terribly painful.

Once back in the office Frank said: 'Well, Aggie knew the name all right, but she weren't going to say anything about it. Mebbe she would have if you hadn't been there – I don't know. I can have another go some time when I meet her without you, but now that she's shut up she may stay that way.

'Only thing I'd say to you – she said "dirty man" in relation to a question about a female. There've been rumours for a while that someone on the staff here – possibly more than one – has been having his way wi' some of the patients. But I couldn't give you any names.'

Christiane said: 'Thanks very much, Frank. We owe you for this. We'd better make tracks now.'

'My pleasure entirely – I don't get many visitors in a place like this. As you're going out, if you happen to see a little man on the front lawn barking like a dog from behind a tree, that'll be Ramon. Just go towards him and then let out a loud "WOOF" as deep as you can. You'll absolutely make his day!'

'We met him on the way in, only we didn't know what to do.'

'Ay, well, yer do now.' And he stared hard at me and said: 'And you take good care of Christina, mate. She's a real decent lassie.'

I grinned. 'I know.'

CHRISTIANE

One night we obviously both felt like being sociable. I'd decided to cook an omelette to prove that I could do it as well as Philip. When I invited him to join me he accepted quite readily. He looked a bit tired and dispirited, and I thought a chat over food might lift things.

We had plenty of eggs, so I got some together and selected herbs and other bits to tang them up a bit. I told Philip to grate some cheese – I thought it might liven him up a little to have something to do.

We decided to sit first at the kitchen table with a glass of wine – an Australian pinot noir which Philip had found somewhere, that proved to be very drinkable.

I told Philip that I'd just heard from a very dear cousin in France that she was in the throes of breaking up her engagement, and she was feeling quite devastated. I said:

'Love's wonderful when it all goes well, but it can tear you apart when it all collapses. I should know – I've been through it enough times myself. Though none was harder than the last one, with Giampaolo.'

There was a bit of a silence, then Philip said:

'I guess I wouldn't really know. I've never been in love or been loved myself. I must say it frightens me rather when I see it happening to other people.'

I was initially speechless, with horror. Never to have been in love or loved by anyone at his age was appalling. I said:

'Surely your parents at least must have loved you, if nobody else?'

'I never thought my father did – he regarded me and my sister as inconvenient nuisances. I guess my mother did, though she was a bit volatile and it was hard to be sure some of the time. But she died when I was twelve, and after that there was nothing. I suppose it's my fault really, but I just don't know how to get started. I panic when I have to show my feelings, and nothing ever gets anywhere.'

I couldn't think of anything else to say. I did notice that Philip didn't seem too concerned at having raised this – he said it quite matter-of-factly, and then moved on to some current news on flooding in south west England, which he said was where he grew up. Then he said: 'I need to go out tomorrow and get some new clothes – shirts and trousers at least. I never know what to get, and I know women have a better feel for what's right. Would you have any thoughts on what I should be looking for?'

Trying very hard to cope with all these changes of subject, I thought I'd better dive in on this God-given chance to get Philip better dressed than he seems to be able to do himself. Which wouldn't be difficult.

'Well, if you like I could come out with you. It's a bit hard to recommend anything when you don't know what's around. I'd promise not to force you into anything – just offer recommendations, and neutral opinions if you try something on.'

I hoped that didn't sound too pushy – that'll come a bit more when we're in the shops....

'That's very kind of you – I'd really appreciate it. Tomorrow morning, as it's Saturday?'

'You're on.'

Whoopee.

We needed another glass of wine after that. Then I whipped up the omelette, which Philip ate with plenty of enthusiasm. He seemed to have brightened up a bit since we sat down, but I still couldn't help thinking of what he'd said about never being loved, which quite horrified me.

Lying in bed that night it was still on my mind. I realised that it probably explains why Philip never seems outgoing when it comes to interactions with people. They – like me at first – take it for indifference and lack of interest, whereas I'm beginning to suspect that he's simply never developed an understanding of how to interact with people and relate to them. Which is actually quite tragic for someone who's basically a nice person. He isn't uninteresting, either - he just needs some way to get him out of himself.

* * *

Next day I didn't know what I was going to be in for with the shopping expedition, but it actually went off very well. We went into four shops in all, and Philip made purchases in two of them. Each time he picked something old-fashioned first. I then said that that might be okay, but let's also try this one, and I picked something more stylish but tried not to sound too pushy.

And I think that my choices were not bad. He does have a good figure and stands well, and he looked – well, dashing's probably a bit strong, but he does have a bit of style when he dresses well.

Luckily on each occasion he also liked my alternative when he tried it on. Let's hope that in the cold light of home they're still all right by him.

SERGEANT NIELSEN

Jimmy Garfield's been chasing up a few more of the vaguely possible suspects for the murder that he found from the newspaper reports of the trial, and he came to see me about one of them this morning.

'You'll love this one, Sarge. I've been recording the interviews I've done with the names on the list I put together. Just listen to this one with Reuben Hardcastle.'

He turned on the tape machine.

GARFIELD: 'Sir, you'll have heard that Rosemary Mason, who you would have known as Rhonda Miller, was murdered some weeks ago. We're interviewing all the people who made statements after her trial saying that she deserved more punishment than she received. Could you please tell me where you were and what you were doing on the tenth of June this year?'

HARDCASTLE: 'I say unto you, on the day of judgment men will give account for every careless word that they speak.'

GARFIELD: 'Thank you, sir, but I wasn't after any careless words – just where you were on the tenth of June.'

HARDCASTLE: 'Whosoever sheds man's blood, by man shall his blood be shed. He that killeth any man shall surely be put to death.'

GARFIELD: 'Er, does that mean that you did shed Rosemary Mason's blood, sir?'

HARDCASTLE: 'Vengeance is mine; I will repay, saith the Lord. The wages of sin is death.'

GARFIELD: 'Sir, please answer my question. Where were you on the tenth of June, and did you kill Rosemary Mason?'

HARDCASTLE: 'I answer to no man, but to a higher authority that sitteth in heaven. I know that my redeemer liveth.'

GARFIELD: 'Sir, I must ask you again – did you have any involvement in the death of Rosemary Mason, and where were you on the tenth of June?'

HARDCASTLE: [silence]

'I couldn't get another word out of him, Sarge. I couldn't mek out if he were takin' the piss or if he were a complete nutter. I think I'd go for nutter rather than the other, but that doesn't mean that he couldn't be a murderer as well.'

'Shit, we're not making a lot of progress on this case, are we? Not your fault, mate, but Inspector Brady's going to have our balls if we don't get somewhere soon. We'll definitely have to keep this bloke on the possible list. Maybe we can dig out a reverend – the police chaplain or someone – who could talk to him on behalf of God. He obviously doesn't want to speak to us mortals.'

AGGIE RANSOME

One reason why I can't ever forget Uncle Bertie and what he did to me is that I know a few of the men staff here are taking the same advantage of some of the patients as my uncle did of me. And if I wasn't able to stop him, how much chance do the poor women here have?

Most of the staff are pretty good on the whole. Some try hard; some are a bit lazy and just do the minimum that they have to, but a few definitely get up to things that they shouldn't with patients. It mostly happens at night, but I don't sleep well – never have since I came here – and I wander around a bit at night.

The one I noticed first was Mr Harrington, the charge nurse on Franklin Ward. He used to take one of his patients into an area with a bed that couldn't be seen from the rest of the ward, and do to them what Uncle Bertie did with me. There was a window from the outside, and I could see it all from that.

I didn't know if I could do anything – I'm sure that nobody would have taken the word of a patient over that of a nurse, just like they wouldn't take mine over Uncle Bertie's. But before I could think if I could do anything Mr Harrington had a heart attack and died, so that was that.

I haven't been quite so sure about the others, but I've got my strong suspicions. Mr Chalmers in Helme Ward looks at some of his patients in funny ways, and when I've been in the ward to empty the waste bins he's been in a backroom with one of the patients, and funny noises have been coming out of there.

Mr Serkin who came after Mr Harrington in Franklin was another I was suspicious of, but then he moved to another hospital so I was never sure about him.

The next one I noticed was Mr Slater from Mansfield Ward. He's a dirty man who's had his way with quite a few patients over the years. He's got a little room at the end of his ward that's never used but it's got two beds in it. He does it mostly at night, but even occasionally during the day. I went into the ward to empty the bins once, and I heard these noises from the little room. I peeped round the door and saw them at it. And I've seen and heard it at other times, with various patients.

I've had my suspicions about one or two other staff as well, but I don't have any evidence on them. And I still don't know what to do about any of it. I feel sorry for the patients that it's happening to, but I hope that some of them at least are too simple to realise what it's all about.

I feel really sick and angry that it reminds me all the time of Uncle Bertie, and I feel even sicker at what must have happened to Rosemary Mason. I saw her that night a few weeks ago when she came into the hospital grounds and went into the main building. I suspected that she was going to see Mr Slater because that's who did it to her before, but I couldn't follow her.

Then I went to the little window at the end of the ward, and peering in I saw something on the bed with Mr Slater on top of it. I'm pretty sure it was her, but it was too dark to see for sure.

Then when I heard that a woman was found dead on the railway just near here, I had the most horrible thoughts. I didn't know at the time that it was Rosemary Mason, but then somebody told me. I've never slept well since I've been here, but it's even worse now. Awful dreams about what might have happened.

PHILIP

My fracture after the run-in with Giampaolo has healed fully now, and my mind's been going back to my other disaster – my attempt to play squash against Christiane. I still think I was a better player than I looked on that day, but my game does need a lot of sharpening up.

Then I thought of James Allworthy in the History Department. I know he's a good squash player, and I'd helped him a little while ago with some negotiations he had with the university on his tenure, so I reckoned he might feel he owes me and be prepared to give me a game or two and some helpful hints.

And I think it worked pretty well. We played twice, quite intensely, and he made various comments on what I could be doing better, and suggested a few strategies for dominating the court a bit more than I had been.

At the end he assured me that I'd sharpened up quite a lot, so I thought I'd ask Christiane if she'd like to have another game.

When I suggested it she said nothing for a moment, and her expression suggested that she was going to ask why I should think I'd be any better than last time, but in the end there was just a slight shrug and she said: 'Okay'.

* * *

We couldn't play for several days, and in the meantime I was beginning to think this was a stupid idea after all. However, backing out would have been complete defeat and we went ahead with it.

And I'd have to say that I was quite pleased in the end at how I went. Christiane still won every game, but I'd expected that. However, this time I got several points off her in each game, and in one I got five points. I also thought that I was getting more of the centre of the court than on the previous occasion, when she'd dominated the centre completely.

At the end she said to me: 'I don't quite know how it came about, but your game's certainly lifted a lot.' She grinned. 'If this goes on I'll have to watch to my laurels. And thank you for an enjoyable match!'

I felt then that I'd restored a bit of dignity after my humiliating performance on the first occasion – not just the defeat but my reaction afterwards.

It was as good as a win.

CHRISTIANE

That night in bed I kept thinking of the squash game with Philip today. He'd improved quite markedly, and I can't work out how that would have happened. It wasn't just that he had an unusually bad game the first time he played me – I could tell that that was his level of play then. I can only think he must have had a bit of coaching from somewhere now, and it certainly showed.

And I thought 'Good for him'. This person who I've kept thinking of as withdrawn, with no "go", has apparently shaken himself out of the torpor and actually done something.

Maybe there's hope for him after all….

SERGEANT NIELSEN

I was having trouble getting hold of my top suspects for Rosemary Mason's murder. Everyone must have been out Christmas shopping or something. Or done a bunk because they were guilty, but I hoped not that. Finally I managed to line up Eberhard Schulz, the founder of the so-called "Men's Justice Movement". I watched as he came into the station and was shown into the interview room. A bulky man with something of a swagger. He was dressed in a darkish suit that had seen better days – obviously trying to present as a sober and responsible citizen. He struck me as a bit smarmy, and I wished he wouldn't keep rubbing his hands. No law against that, though.

Brian Hawkins wasn't available, so Jimmy Garfield was going to do the honours. I told him to do the intro while I watched Schulz.

'Good morning, sir. We're enquiring into the murder of Rosemary Mason, who you knew as Rhonda Miller because you attended her trial when she was accused of the murder of her husband. That trial was a somewhat controversial one, and we're interviewing all the people who took a particular interest in the trial in case they decided to follow that interest through later on.'

Schulz interrupted at that point. 'If you know anything about me you'd know that of course I took an interest in the trial. I represent the interests of men whose point of view's all too often overlooked in modern life. Every bloody thing these days is women's rights, women's lib, give the women all the rights...'

He was just getting a head of steam up, and I thought I'd better cap the steam vent.

'So you disagreed with the verdict from the trial?'

At that he began to puff up. 'It was a travesty of justice! A disgrace to our legal system!' He was shouting. 'She killed her lawfully wedded husband – that can't be anything but murder! She deserved to be executed, only our country in its stupidity has done away with the death penalty.'

'I'm not intending to argue that case with you, but I will point out that her husband had been hitting her regularly and quite severely for a number of years, and it was on that ground that it was found that she'd acted in self defence.'

'Self defence, my foot! She was probably a disobedient wife who was not doing as her husband had told her. That never came out properly at the trial!'

Little flecks of spittle were landing on the table in front of him, and I was pleased that I was sitting out of range. I noticed Jimmy edging back slightly.

'OK sir, given that view, you obviously felt that Rosemary Mason, or Rhonda Miller, should have been put to death. I will ask you formally – did you murder her in order to achieve that end?'

'I most certainly did not. I use only legal means for securing my ends – I mean our ends. Anything else would be counter-productive to our cause, which is the re-establishment of basic rights for men – something that's been entirely lost in recent times...'

Here we go again. 'Sir, I just need to ask you where you were on the night of tenth June last.'

'I assume that that was when Ms Miller was killed.' He thought for a moment. 'I'm pretty sure I was away in Liverpool that night. We had a week's symposium on restoration of men's rights, organised by our national executive. I'd have to check on my diary at home, but I'm fairly sure that was right.'

I debated whether or not to insist that he brought the diary to us, but I thought that I wouldn't mind seeing where he ran his office from.

'OK sir, we could come with you if you don't object. Now?'

'You're welcome. I've got nothing to hide – nothing at all.'

I looked at Jimmy Garfield who nodded, and we set off following Schulz's car. Not a white estate car, incidentally. He drove to a part of Lancaster that was known for its keen support of the Conservative party. His car pulled into a driveway, and we parked in the street outside.

The house, like his suit, had seen better days, but the garden was reasonably neat – it was just the timberwork that had flaking paint and some patches of rot in the wood. His office was obviously home-based.

He waved us into the house and into a front room, which had a desk and swivel chair, two bookshelves overflowing with files, and one rather worn easy chair. The desk was strewn with papers that didn't look very systematically organised. One wall had a large poster showing a man in the centre of the picture, with an idealised and adoring wife beside and slightly behind him, and then two smiling children in front. One boy and one girl, the boy of course the older one. The wife had an apron on. The slogan across the top read "The Family that Lives Together is a Happy Family!". Vintage about the nineteen fifties, I would guess.

Schulz dug around on his desk for a while. I would have expected the diary to be easily accessible for use, but it eventually appeared from well down in the humus layer.

'Now, what was the date that you were after?'

'The tenth of June last,' said Jimmy patiently.

Schulz flipped the pages. 'June the tenth – no, it wasn't Liverpool – I was at a meeting and then a fete for "Restoration of Family Tradition". I was busy for the entire day.' He waved the diary page at us, and it did indeed show those two items.

'We were actually interested in the night time – say eleven pm to about two or three am.'

'Oh, I'd have been in bed by then. I don't go out late anywhere.'

'So you don't actually have an alibi for the time when the murder was committed?'

'This is ridiculous – I've already told you that I had nothing to do with it and I never saw her again after the trial.'

'Would your wife or family be able to corroborate that you were home and asleep at the relevant time?'

'I, erm – I don't have a wife, and my children have left home. But I can assure you that I never stay up late in the evenings.'

In other words he had no relevant alibi, and he was in fact in Lancaster on the day in question. However, there was little point in pursuing the questions further in the absence of any specific evidence pointing towards him, so I thought we might as well leave.

I glanced at Jimmy, who pursed his lips, then nodded his head towards the door.

'Thank you, sir, for your time in this matter.'

'My pleasure – any time I can help officers of the law just let me know.'

We walked to our car in the street and sat there for a moment.

"Pompous git,' said Jimmy.

'No argument with that. I wanted to get that reference to his wife in because I didn't think there was any sign of a woman or woman's influence round the house. And there isn't, obviously. What do you make of all this stuff about traditional families and he doesn't have one?'

'I reckon she saw the light and walked out on him. Wouldn't blame her. But whether that makes him murder other women to get revenge I wouldn't know. I've heard of stranger things than that.'

'Well, the calendar only has two daytime activities, so he's not in the clear. Maybe we should check a bit further on this Men's Justice Movement – see how many other people belong to it, if it does even exist. See if there's a national executive – that sort of thing.'

'I don't know. I've never heard of that one before, and he's doing this on our patch. Maybe we should follow it up after all. That organisation mightn't exist outside his head, and maybe he did it after all. Could you please follow that one up a bit?'

'Okay, Sarge. It's good of you to give me all the plum jobs. I really enjoyed this one. Yuck, I really don't like guys like that.'

'Well, it's because you're so good at it that you get them. Don't worry. There may be a pint in it at the end, if you're lucky. Meanwhile there's a few more charmers we have to interview. Let's go.'

He didn't bother to grace that one with a reply – just an eye-roll.

CHRISTIANE

One of our technicians in the computer centre was selling cakes today to raise money for a campaign to reduce domestic violence against women. Such a theme had to be very close to my heart, so I bought a generous selection.

Next day was Saturday, so I served them instead of our usual biscuits for morning tea at home.

'We had a cake drive at work yesterday to raise funds for a program to fight domestic violence against women. You have to eat some of these – I'll force-feed you if necessary.'

'No compulsion – I'm more than happy to eat as many as I can. With all my exposure to you and Giampaolo, and Rosemary Mason and her husband, not to mention some others in the press lately, I've been thinking a lot about that. It just appals me to think of what the victims must go through, but you'd know all about that.'

'You've said it. It absolutely blights a person's life, and once it's started you never get away from it. You never know from one minute to the next whether the perpetrator's going to lash out again, or rather when it's going to happen, not if. You dread going home, and when you're there and nothing's happening, you don't ever know whether it's just about to explode. The endless tension's terrible.

'You lose any social life and friends because you spend all your time looking out for violence, and not really knowing what's going to trigger it. The unpredictability's one of the worst things. The physical pain's bad enough, but the mental stress is even worse. And one of the awful things mentally is that you can actually begin to think after a while that maybe it's your fault not his.

'Then if you finally take some steps to stop it with a restraining order or something it doesn't necessarily end, as you'll have noted with me and Paolo. In the end you almost wonder whether you'd be better off dead than living a life of endless tension.'

'I can totally understand all of that, and it horrifies me even more. All I can say in your case the cycle may finally have been broken, and despite the run-in with Giampaolo a few weeks ago I think you can finally start feeling safe again here. I hope…?'

'You're right, and I'm hugely grateful for that. I did actually begin to feel safe at Mrs Marshall's. Her house wasn't in the sort of area where Paolo would have found me all that readily, and even if he had I suspect Mrs Marshall would have been a match for him. You didn't meet her, but she was a large and solid lady with enormous beefy arms, and I reckon she could have walloped him pretty effectively. She certainly wouldn't have taken any nonsense from anyone. That arrangement ended of course when she needed my room, but I've felt quite safe here and I've really loved it. That's why I was so devastated when

Paolo did find me here again. What had seemed like the final sanctuary became threatened again.'

'Well that didn't last, thank God. I do believe that you're safe here now, and Aunt Clarissa can replace Mrs Marshall in watching over you. And me as well, for what that's worth.'

'Don't keep talking yourself down, Philip. That's worth a lot, believe me. I haven't really told you enough how much I've been enjoying living here and I should have. When I came first to inspect the place and you said that you were proposing to let the top floor, I thought "Oh my God, an attic". Then when I climbed the stairs and saw the two rooms I couldn't believe my eyes. It's one of the nicest places I've ever lived in. It's far nicer than your own bedroom, I'd have to say.'

'Well, I'd actually have to agree with you there. When I first acquired the house I thought of making the top part my living area, but then I decided that it'd be selfish to have a house this size all to myself and I'd let part of it. And I thought that a tenant might feel funny if they had me coming past their rooms all the time, so I went into my current area.'

'I must tell you one other thing that I love, which is the steep and twisting staircase up to my area. You know how in many English churches the tower has similar stairs up to the top, also with the stairs twisting clockwise so that an enemy raiding the church has to approach defenders with his sword in his left hand – well, our staircase reminds me very much of one of those.

'And while I'm letting it all spill out, I should add that I've very much enjoyed your company since I've been here. When I was an undergraduate I used to have a great social life, until I got married. Then my social life revolved around Paolo, and when that went wrong I had no social life at all. And even when I took out the order against him, I had to live as quietly and hidden away as I could so I still couldn't socialise. Mrs Marshall was never more than a daunting landlady, and life was pretty lonely till I came here. Since I've been here I've enjoyed your company a lot – quite a few different aspects of it. As I said before you shouldn't talk yourself down so much – you're better than that.'

'Thank you – in all honesty I think that's more than I deserve, but it's accepted gratefully. And can I say that you've also done me wonders since you've been here. I greatly enjoy your company, and you've got me trying all sorts of things I've never done before, like cooking new dishes, baking things and so on. Even teaching me not to iron bedsheets…

'And as a tailpiece, I'll add that you can feel safe here with not only Aunt Clarissa and me looking after you, but also Sergeant Nielsen. He's got Giampaolo firmly down in his books now, and if he does show his face back here the Sergeant wants to question him about what he did to me and the hallstand. And I've noticed the Sergeant's one of your admirers too, so he's certainly not going to let anything happen to you.'

'Thank you again, Philip. I think we definitely ought to have another cake to sign off on all of that….'

FRANK ELLIOTT

I were thinkin' about what Christina and her lad were sayin' about that poor lady that were killed near here. I had a niece who were killed by a man that she met at a party, and I saw the terrible things that it does to a family when that happens.

Ever since then I've wanted to do summat to stop this sort of thing, but I don't really know if I can or not. I'm not a detective or anything. Old Aggie knows summat, but I'll likely never get anything out of her now that she's been asked and said she didn't know. But I'll mention to some of the lads around the place that if they find anything odd in any way they should let me know. You just never know when something might come up. The poor lass were found right close to here, and maybe summat did happen in the hospital after all. I wish I could get Aggie to say summat but she won't.

I mentioned it to some of the porters. They were sympathetic about the poor lass but you could see that they didn't think owt'd be found by the likes of us. Leave it to the police, they said – they're the experts. I told the gardeners as well, because they're always poking around the grounds. Old Herbie had a bit of a chuckle. He said: 'You want to know if there's owt strange around here? Every bloody thing we find here's strange! You wouldn't believe what some o' them patients hide around the place. But don't worry – if there's anything that does strike me I'll let you know. Bit o' luck and I might get you to do half me work for me!'

I told young Tommy Arkwright about it too. Me and Tommy work together a bit because he does the drains and I have to go into the drains for the cockroaches and the rats. Tommy said I'd know perfectly well what he'd be mostly finding – the clothing that some of the dafter patients in the locked wards flush down the toilets. Most of the time they don't go anywhere, but every now and then they get a run on and Tommy's fishin' down one of the manholes to get 'em out again.

It's one way to mek a living, I suppose. Me, I'll stick wi' the rats and cockroaches.

SERGEANT NIELSEN

I've managed to catch up with Frank Higginbotham, another one of the main suspects for Rosemary Mason's murder, so I hauled Brian Hawkins in yet again.

'The next guy I've called in for interview should be here at the station in a few minutes. I've read the report on him from the time of the trial, and it doesn't make very nice reading.

'Mason's husband had done his wife serious injury on more than one occasion. However, Higginbotham yelled out at the end of the trial that it was up to husbands what they did with their wives, and she had no excuse in law to kill him – she should have just put up with what he did. He also yelled out that she was guilty as hell and she should hang. He called all this out in court, and he was ejected for his pains.'

'Sounds like another good one, Sarge.'

'Would you like to take the running this time, and I'll watch and intervene when appropriate?'

'OK by me, Sarge.'

I wasn't at the trial so I didn't know what to expect, but I'd thought maybe a large and thuggish man with a belligerent manner. However, in the flesh he looked quite normal – not heavy, and no obvious hints of aggressiveness. However, when he spoke it was a different matter.

Brian started the interview off.

'Good morning, sir. You may have heard that someone called Rosemary Mason was murdered recently. You knew her as Rhonda Miller, and we're interviewing all the people who made threats against her during her trial. One of those was you….'

He didn't give Brian time to finish.

'She deserved all she got. She was an evil woman. The Bible says that a woman shall serve her husband. If she doesn't then the husband has a right to step in and make her do what she should do. She should have been hanged.'

'Since you feel that way about it, were you the person who murdered her as you'd threatened at the trial?'

'No, I wasn't and there's no bloody way you're going to pin that one on me.'

'Sir, I have to ask you then where you were on Saturday tenth of June?'

He frowned and said nothing for a minute or two; then I saw a smirk cross his face.

'I was in custody, wasn't I? I was dragged in because I was suspected of assaulting a woman who I didn't even know. You lot should know that if anyone does. I was in the nick for two days and then they released me because they had no evidence. And I've heard that they got someone else for it later anyway. That was police harassment of me yet again.'

That was a black mark against me because I should have

looked up his record before the interview.

'Okay, which nick were you in so I can check?'

'Preston. Bastards the lot of 'em.'

'One final question, sir. What make and colour of car do you drive?'

'It's an old Land Rover, sort of dull brown, and before you ask all the bloody papers are in order for it.'

'Thank you, sir. That will be all for now.'

He went out muttering "I should bloody think so. Fucken' cops always after a bloke…"

'Jesus, I'm sorry about that, Brian – my fault. I just didn't check his record before he came in or I'd have spotted that.'

'No worries, Sarge. It never hurts to see what sorts of low-lifes are out there, even if they're not the ones that you want right at the moment.'

I was cross at myself, and I also had an unpleasant taste in my mouth after meeting Frank Higginbotham – one of the nastier people I've met in recent times. I was certainly going to check out his alibi. If it held up then I'd have to cross him off the list of suspects, but that would be a great disappointment.

TOMMY ARKWRIGHT

I knew it were going to be a bad day even before I got to work. I got pissed last night, and I still felt pissed when I got up this morning. Then I dropped the coffee jar – the only one with any in – and when I went outside I saw the scrape on the side of the car. Vague memory of how that happened, but pretty vague.

When I got to work – a bit late – there were already two notes pinned to my door. Bloody Bassingthwaite Upper reckoned their toilets were flooding again, and I only done 'em yesterday. The other one was the toilets attached to the recreation hall. That one were unusual. There's nowt to stop patients flushing clothes down those ones like all the other toilets, but the sorts of patients who do the flushing are mostly the really daft ones in the locked wards, and they don't ever get out to the hall.

I thought Bassingthwaite Upper can wait – I'll do the rec hall first. But as soon as I opened the door there was a call from the operating room – drains needed urgent cleaning – and I allus has to give that priority.

That took me till nearly lunchtime because they did have a real problem, so it weren't till afternoon that I got to the hall.

It didn't take too long to find the problem. There were various bits of women's clothing that must have been flushed down the loo, and as luck would have it they banked up on one of the sharp bends just outside the back door. There was a convenient access cover there, and I were able to get 'em out quite easily. They were a bit clarted oop wi' muck from the drain, but they'd clean up okay.

Bit funny what they were, too. I can recognise the sorts of clobber that all the patients wear, and these weren't like them. They were pretty smart women's clothing – panties, a bra, a sweatshirt, some long trousers and socks. No shoes that I could see, though they could have gone down first and not got stuck.

I thought about this for a minute or two, and then I remembered Frank Elliott talking about the bird who were found on the railway line near here. He were saying that she might have had some connection with this place. I couldn't very well leave the clothes lying around – someone might have just cleared 'em away, or worse a patient might have picked 'em up and done God knows what with 'em. Put 'em on, mebbe. So I marked the spot outside with some stones that wouldn't get moved around, and took the clobber back to me workshop. Then I rang Frank but he weren't in, so I went and poked a note under his door.

CHRISTIANE

It was Saturday morning and I was in the cellar washing some clothes when Philip called down the steps: 'Please stay in for coffee this morning – I've got some special biscuits. Guaranteed not a shortbread in sight!'

It sounded intriguing, and I was intending to be there anyway. Anything after the excitement of doing loads of washing....

At the appointed hour Philip was just setting the coffee maker up, and there was a plate heaped with small round biscuits, each light brown in colour and with a half almond baked into the top.

Philip said: 'I have to share these because I think they're rather nice. I tried one when I was given them at work yesterday.'

'How come you were given these at work?'

'I'll tell you when we eat them.'

All very mysterious, but I could wait.

In due course the coffee was served, and I tried a biscuit. It was crisp and light at the same time, and had a deliciously nutty flavour – not simply from the almond on the top but it must have been through the whole biscuit.

'These are lovely. I think they must have some sort of nut flavour through the flour – it can't be just from the nut on top.'

'I was told that there's some almond meal in the mixture – quite a lot, I'd say. It certainly does make them tasty.'

'Right, now you have to share the mystery of their origin!'

'Well, they came completely out of the blue, but I suppose you could say they're an unexpected perk of working in the staffing office.

'One of my roles is to select workplace harassment contacts and get the chosen people trained, and in order to do that properly I've had to undergo the training myself. I'm not formally down as a contact, but every now and then I get people coming to me with their problems regardless. They seem to think that if I'm in Staffing I must do everything. I try to deflect them off to the appointed contacts, but I had one lady a while ago who just said: "I'm not actually coming about harassment, at least not of the workplace sort, but I've got a problem and I'm desperate to talk to someone about it. I'd just like a human being to talk to, and you seemed human when you interviewed me for my job here".

'I suppose it was the fact that somebody actually thought I was human that did it, though I also felt sorry for her as she sounded pretty desperate. I thought it couldn't do any harm at least to listen to her – I could then pass her on as appropriate.

'She told me that her problem was with her elderly parents. Her father had dementia to the point that he didn't even know which planet he was on – her words. He was still living at his home, and her mother was trying her best to look after him, but when someone's that bad it's a hell of a lot of work, and her mother wasn't in the best of physical health either.

'She told me that she'd said many times to her mother that she should either get help or put the father into a suitable home, but the mother was strongly – and literally violently – opposed to that. The situation was getting worse and worse, so she went to the authorities to see what could be done. They told her that they couldn't do anything without the mother's permission, unless the situation became a public nuisance or a threat to safety or something.

'She tried again with her mother, who screamed at her, grabbed her and shook her. In the end she had to give up because she didn't want to distress her mother even more, but at the same time something clearly had to be done.

'Finally she said: "Thank you for listening to me so patiently. I didn't expect you to have any solutions, but I just wanted to share it all with someone. I don't have any sisters or brothers. My husband and I parted some years ago, and we didn't have any children. I just didn't know anyone else who might be prepared to listen".

'I said: "Look, you're right that I can't do anything directly, and it's not a situation that I've had any personal experience with, but one idea does occur to me. One of the medical specialists who the university calls on every now and then is actually an expert on old-age problems. I'll contact her and ask her if she wouldn't mind talking to you".

'When I contacted the doctor I mentioned how I thought this was quite a serious case, and she said she'd be happy to see my person. That was the last I heard of it until yesterday. Then my person came back to me, looking much more cheerful than before, and said: "You won't believe it, but my father's now in quite a nice nursing home where he seems to be happy. My mother visits him often and they sit together. Sometimes she pushes him in a wheelchair round the garden. And better still, she gets a little help at home now because of her increasing infirmities.

'When I went to talk to your doctor she told me what strategy we had to use to approach my mother in order to get her to agree to anything, and she then organised a three-way meeting of herself, my mum and me. She was magic, and I'm so grateful to you for doing this for me. Here's a very small token of my appreciation, which I baked myself.'

'She gave me the biscuits that you're eating. I tried one on the spot and it was lovely, though I still think the best reward was that someone thought I might be human.'

'Well, the biscuits certainly are very nice – she's obviously a really good baker. And on the humanity side, I've sort of been trying to tell you that for a while now. Obviously not effectively enough!'

'I know you have, and I'm grateful for that too. I might even get to believe it myself one day. In the meantime, have another biscuit!'

SERGEANT NIELSEN

Jimmy Garfield had nearly run down all his list of people with white estate cars in the area. He'd got a couple of names that were still possible because their alibis were rather vague, but neither seemed very likely either. There were two others that he couldn't find, but all the evidence suggested that they were no longer in the area. Their names were down as having cars in this area, but that meant very little.

Brian and I, however, were about to interview another of the significant suspects, Dermot O'Leary. I gave Brian the background.

'This will be Dermot O'Leary when he gets here. He didn't shout out threats or anything at the trial, but he attended every day of the trial and he was noted as staring very intently at Rosemary Mason during the proceedings and making copious notes on a pad of paper that he had with him. He wasn't a reporter or anything, and he wasn't known to be an author. The trial notes said that his interest seemed a bit unhealthy.

'After the stuff-up with Frank Higginbotham I've checked O'Leary's record carefully. He's had a number of prosecutions for stalking and harassing single women. He generally pestered them for sex, but he hasn't ever physically assaulted any of them as far as the records show. However, during police interviews he's shown general hostility towards women, and he's made some quite menacing comments. I think it'll be another rather unpleasant interview coming up.'

Again I hadn't ever encountered him before the interview. When he was shown in I noted casual but neat dress. He sat in front of us looking relaxed and unworried.

Brian kicked it off again.

'Sir, you may be aware of the recent murder of someone called Rosemary Mason. That wasn't her original name – she was previously known as Rhonda Miller, and you were noted to have been a regular observer at her trial when she was charged with murdering her husband who'd been beating her frequently.'

'Aye, well I take an interest in crime stories and the legal processes, and that was an interesting trial. If I remember right she was acquitted on the grounds that it was self-defence. But I didn't know she'd been murdered. Tragic really. Maybe someone who didn't agree with the verdict did for her. Not sure if I could blame them really – there was a lot of controversy about the result at the time.'

It was all a bit too pat – he must have known what questions might be coming and he was ready for them. I didn't like the slightly smug expression on his face as he delivered it all, and there was a touch of arrogance too. Time to stir a bit harder, so I chipped in.

'Sir, we're interviewing anyone involved with the trial who also has a record of menacing behaviour towards women. Your record shows that you've been prosecuted a number of times for stalking women and generally harassing them.'

His face had hardened as I said that.

'If you know that you'd know that I was never charged with hurting any of the women. Maybe I did get a bit carried away putting the hard word on ones I was attracted to, but it was never more than that. As your records must show.' He glared at us then.

'Aye, well, there've been plenty of cases where stalkers have upped their aggression when they've felt they weren't getting anywhere. And who knows, you might have had a particular problem with that trial – after all it was an aggressive male who got his comeuppance.'

'Well, I didn't and you can't have any proof that I was involved. If you have, then show me. And tell me when the murder occurred and I'll try to tell you where I was and what I was doing at the time. I think you're trying to bluff me.'

He was looking cross and sounding somewhat aggressive, but I didn't get any feeling that he was showing any signs of worry.

'Sir, where were you on the night of Saturday tenth of June?'

He looked genuinely blank, and I felt that if he'd known that he'd have been ready for it as he was with the earlier questions. He thought for several minutes.

'I'm pretty certain that that was the weekend when I went to London. I stayed at the Bell Hotel in Finsbury Park. You can check with them that I had a room then. And I had dinner in the hotel, so that should be in their records and all.'

'Thank you, sir – yes, we'll check it out. And one final question – what sort of car do you drive?'

'A Ford Fiesta.'

'Colour?'

'Bright red – like a pillar box.'

I looked at Brian, who shrugged. He didn't seem to think we were getting any traction either.

'Thank you, sir – you can go now. We'll check out the London hotel in due course.'

He gave us a stony look, and got up and left without another word.

'Another charmer, but I'm not sure that I see him as all that likely for this one. If he was guilty I think he'd have had an immediate alibi for the date and time. Though it could have been a bluff too – sounding all innocent.'

'I didn't see him as a real prospect either, Sarge.'

Thinking about it after I couldn't really see him as a strong suspect. He was an unpleasant person, but this just didn't quite seem to fit with him.

PHILIP

It's getting close to Christmas, and I need to know what Christiane's intending to do in the break. When she came in from work I asked her: 'Are you planning to go away for Christmas or anything – family or something?'

'I hadn't really thought about it – we've been so busy at work lately. I don't think family's an option at the moment. Would it worry you if I did stay here?'

'Absolutely not, and it's your flat to live in anyway. And I'd welcome another person in the house. When you're little, Christmas is always a time with lots of people around, and it's never as much fun alone.' I did a bit of quick thinking. 'If you don't mind I might try to cook a traditional Christmas dinner. That's another Christmas memory, but I've never done one before because there's never seemed much point for just one person.'

'Mm, that's a nice idea – I'll be in that.'

'That's good because I was going to ask you for one bit of help. I reckon I can do it all except for the bread sauce, and I know you're a great sauce chef....'

She gave me a look that suggested she might have been conned, but she said: 'Okay, it's a deal.'

We agreed that the meal would be on the Sunday that was the actual Christmas Day, and I began to think of the menu and what I would need to buy. We never had turkey when I was small, and I don't know that a whole turkey would fit into our oven, so roast chicken, roast potatoes and parsnips, a green vegetable and gravy would probably be the menu. With Christiane's bread sauce, of course. It's far too late to make a Christmas pudding now, but I hope I'm up to baking some mince pies that are edible.

FRANK ELLIOTT

When I got to work this morning I found a note under me door which seemed to be from young Tommy Arkwright. His writing isn't the best, nor his spelling neither, but it seemed to be to do with some clothes that he'd found in a drain near the recreation hall. I wasn't sure if he wanted me to treat the area, so I picked up rat baits, made up some cockroach spray and headed off to find him.

But when I found him he told me that he'd never had this problem with the rec hall before, and the clothes weren't the usual sort that get flushed away so he was thinking they might have had something to do with the woman who was killed. I wasn't sure then what to do, but I said I'd come back to his room and have a look at them.

When I saw 'em I thought he might well be right, but I was out of me depth with that sort of thing. I told Tommy to hang on to 'em and not let anyone get near them, and I rang Christina at her work. She said to leave it with her – she'd contact the police. That had me wondering then what I should do about the hospital. They weren't going to like the police marching in and saying that we'd called 'em all by ourselves. In the end I decided that I'd wait until the police were arriving and then tell the boss that I'd just rung the police for advice and they insisted on coming straight round. They still wouldn't like it but I didn't think they could do much. There aren't enough trained pest controllers around to sack me.

Don't much like the cops meself, but Christina reckons the one she's talking to's OK, and I'm doing it for her. I've got a soft spot for yon lass.

* * *

When the police arrived I felt better about it – it were me old mate Len Nielsen. Him and me used to play darts at the Fox and Goose a few years back. I was going to let young Tommy have his moment of glory telling Len how he'd found the stuff, but it turned out that he wasn't at all keen on talking to the cops – some other offence in the offing, I'd guess. So I had to do the honours, and I explained to him how and where they were found.

'So how come pest control officers are getting involved with murder enquiries these days?'

'It were through this lass Christina – she tells me she's been talking to you she. She said she's been helping you a bit with what you were doing.'

'Yes well, I wouldn't quite put it like that – leastways not while my inspector's listening. But she's a bright lass and she's made some useful comments. So how do you know her?'

'I've known her for a few years. I do some part-time pest control at the university office where she works, and she's my contact there. And she's one of the best, I can tell you. Not so sure about the young feller she lives with, but.'

'I'll agree with you on Ms Guchez, but young Philip's not so bad either. You know that Ms Guchez was beaten up by her ex a while ago?'

'Aye, she did tell me that. He sounded like a real bastard. The ex, I mean.'

'He was, I think. Anyway, when Philip heard about that she warned him that he might get the same if the ex came back. She was going to move out, but he said no, he'd cope and she wasn't to give in to that sort of bullying.'

'And did it happen?'

'Yes, it did, and no he didn't cope but it wasn't really his own fault. He tripped as he stepped backwards in his hallway and fell over. I think the ex did hit him, but he was mostly beaten up by his own hallstand which fell and broke on top of him. Anyway, he's a bit quiet but his heart's in the right place. And it looks as though the ex has finally scarpered from this area. Good riddance to the bugger, too.'

'So what do you want to do wi' these clothes? We get plenty of bits of clothing flushed down toilets all the time here, but they're never like this. They're usually rather shabby and old, but these are quite smart. A bit slutched oop from the drains, but you could clean that off. Young Tommy reckons this didn't come from any of the patients, and I've never seen patients wearing stuff like this, neither. If you want we can get the head sewing lady to offer a comment too. She knows all the patients' clothing.'

'Aye well, that mightn't be a bad idea if we can do it soon.'

'I'll give her a ring now.'

I came back to say she was on her way now.

'I think she was rather taken by the idea of being part of a crime investigation. Life isn't all that exciting in a loony bin sewing room most of the time.'

Right on cue a middle-aged woman strode up, half-glasses perched on the end of her nose and an expectant expression all over her face. She was introduced as Molly. She stared at the heap of clothing.

'Can I touch them?'

'If you put these gloves on you can. Gently, though.'

Molly pulled each item out in turn and spread it out carefully. She said nothing until the end, then:

'Well, they certainly weren't worn by any patient here, leastways not anyone who's in here at the moment. It's good quality and very little worn. The wearer would have been around five foot or so, and fairly slim. And that's about all I can tell you.'

Len said: 'Thank you – that's a great help. That was about the right size for the lady that was killed near here – it might just be hers. We'll have to follow up on a few other aspects next.'

Molly looked a bit disappointed. She was probably hoping for a longer break from the sewing.

'There's nothing else I can help you with, then?' she asked hopefully.

'No, you've been a great help already,' said Len.

She pursed her lips. I gave her a friendly nod, but she still looked disappointed as she marched off again.

I said to Len: 'Well, I suppose you'll be taking these with you then?'

'Aye. I don't know what chance there is of getting DNA off

clothing that's been in a drain for a few weeks, but they can only try. But we can compare it to the gear that's still in the woman's house – that might give us some idea.

'And then the next step'd be to work out where the stuff could have gone into the drain to finish up here, and who that might point the finger at. That'd need some detailed plans of the drains, and some local expertise.'

He gave me a pointed look.

'We'd need your young mate for that. I don't know what he's done to be so shy of the police, but if it isn't all that bad I'd guess blind eyes might be turned.'

CHRISTIANE

It was Saturday after a hectic week at work, and I thought I'd take things a bit more quietly while I had the chance.

I came down to the kitchen to make some coffee, and found that Philip was there and already had some brewing. When it was ready he poured me a cup and then said:

'I thought you might be getting bored with all the short-bread biscuits I've been making so I've tried something new – ginger biscuits.'

I tried one and it wasn't too bad, though I'd got quite fond of the butteriness of the shortbreads and these didn't quite have the same appeal. I couldn't really say anything, however – I just hoped that he might also like the shortbreads more and go back to them.

He had the Saturday paper open on the kitchen table, and on Saturdays it always has book reviews which was what he seemed to be reading.

'Any good books showing up today?'

'Well, it depends what your interests are. If you're into

fantasy there's an Armageddon blockbuster that's really bloody – I'm not swearing, it sounds like it's full of violence and gore. I can't stand that sort of thing, though. After that a biography of a very forgettable Conservative ex-politician – ditto. A couple of thrillers that may or may not be all right, but they sound a bit pot-boiling. So the answer's probably no, but you're welcome to look for yourself – you may have different tastes.'

'Doesn't sound too encouraging, though I always feel sorry for authors who put all the effort into creating a book and then it gets panned. I've never had any talent at writing myself.'

There was a longish pause, and then Philip said: 'I've actually tried my hand at writing, but it's not finished yet. I've never shown it to anybody, though, so I've no idea what it's like. It's very hard to judge your own work – it all looks perfect to you, and I know it usually isn't.'

I did some very quick thinking here. 'I take your point about it being hard to judge your own work. I could never judge my attempts at art either. My mother seemed to like them, but you couldn't rule out bias there.' I hesitated for a moment. '*If* you ever wanted someone to look at what you've done I'd be prepared to cast my eye over it. It's a big if, of course, and I'm completely inexpert when it comes to what publishers or agents might think, so it's probably not worth it anyway.'

The bait was there....

Philip considered for a minute or two. 'Can I think about that? It's very kind of you to offer, and I know it can be potentially embarrassing because if you think it's awful it can be hard to say that. I'll work on that, but thanks again for the offer.'

Well, it might happen. I'd actually be quite interested to see what he's written. I can't even remotely guess what genre or subject it might be, and it could tell me a bit more about the person that Philip is. Maybe....

SERGEANT NIELSEN

It's not looking good for DNA from the clothing in the hospital drains – they're going to have another go, but they aren't putting any money on it. I've been trying to think of another approach, and it occurred to me to go back to Ms Guchez and ask her to do something for me.

It's sometimes easier to do things face to face, so I went round to her house. Her eyes widened a bit when she opened the door and saw me, but it wasn't hostile. I'd been wondering a bit whether the pair of them might have been getting sick of the police.

'Have you spoken to Frank Elliott recently? You'll probably know that him and his mate found some women's clothing blocking a drain in the hospital, and it didn't look like the usual patient's clothing.'

'Yes, he did mention it to me – I was the one who rang your station for him. He was round at our offices a couple of nights ago, and he told me you'd been round to the hospital and collected the clothes. I was hoping that might give you some clues as to who committed the murder?'

'So were we, but sadly not yet. We'd hoped to get DNA confirmation that the clothing did actually belong to Rosemary Mason, but at this stage no luck. But that isn't the end of it – we can follow up a few other leads still. One is to compare these clothes with other items from Rosemary's wardrobe, for size, style and anything else. That's where I was wondering if you might be able to help me?'

'Me? But shouldn't you be getting a policewoman to do that? I've got no training or experience or anything.'

'In the ordinary way of things yes, but our best WPC left last week for a new job in Bradford. God knows why she'd want to go there, but that's her business. Then the next in line's in bed with a severe attack of measles which she picked up from one of her kids who got it from school, and the last one's on a training course in York. We're a bit light on for gender equality at the moment. But it doesn't matter for something like this. There's no police training that teaches you what I'm after, which is just a good feminine eye and judgement of another woman's clothing.'

I gave her what I hoped was my most encouraging stare. 'That's where I thought you might be the best candidate of all.' Cheesy grin to follow – tried not to overdo it.

She gave me a long stare, probably trying to judge how serious I was. Then she gave me a grin back.

'OK, you're on! I can do it now if you're ready. But would you mind if Philip came along as well? He may not be able to add much, but you never know. He's just upstairs somewhere.'

I don't know if she didn't trust me one on one, but anyway the three of us set out for Rosemary Mason's house. No skin off my nose – I just wanted some answers.

Inside the house I handed out protective gloves for all three of us. 'Please put these on and don't touch any part of the clothing with your bare skin. We need to try and protect the DNA if there's still any there.'

I carefully spread out the clothing from the drain on the main bed, and then opened the wardrobes while the other two watched. I pulled out four pairs of slacks and put them next to the drain pair. Ms Guchez gingerly lifted one of the wardrobe pairs and placed its waistband on top of the other one. It was the same size. She did this with the others – roughly the same result. Then we took out blouses and did similar size matches, and then underwear.

Ms Guchez said: 'My judgement is that these are pretty much the same size, though I don't know that that would be strong evidence in a court of law. Now I suppose we should look at styles to see if they might have been bought by a person with the same tastes.'

We all stared in silence – in my case because I couldn't think of anything to say. I'm not good on that sort of appraisal.

Finally Ms Guchez said: 'I'd be prepared to say that these clothes could well have belonged to the same person as your samples, but I'd also suspect that if you went to someone else's house you might get the same result there. I just can't see this being any use in a court case – I think any reasonable defence counsel could make mincemeat of it.'

'You're quite right, but what it does give me is a stronger reason to go back to the hospital and try to work out how and where the clothing might have got into the drain, and why that particular drain was chosen. It's not one that patients have ever used before, although some of them do have access to it. If I can work through that I might get some idea as to who might have put it in there.'

Philip Dow suddenly spoke. 'It's maybe a bit stronger than that. I interviewed Rosemary Mason and I recall the session quite well. I pay reasonable attention to what people wear at interviews because it tells you a bit about them, and I think your samples are pretty much the sort of thing she was wearing at the interview.' He paused for a moment, and then added: 'We should have got her on CCTV when she came for the interview, too, because there's a camera on the door of the interview room that's on all the time. Not because we want to record interviewees, but it's also the room where one of our main safes is. Unfortunately it's likely that the tape's been wiped by now, but I can go and ask the security staff.'

We agreed that that was all we could do for the moment, pending any further information from the university CCTV.

* * *

Later in the day I had by a phone call from the university – the CCTV footage did still exist after all. I was told that it wouldn't normally have been, but on the same day as the interview there'd been a security incident, and so they'd held on to the footage.

I went to the university's security office where I found Philip Dow and Ms Guchez, and another familiar face.

'How do, Bill. What're you doing in a place like this? Couldn't you handle it in the police force?!'

He'd put on a bit of weight since he left us – they must pay them all right here.

He grinned at me.

'How are yer, Len? Well, it was OK in the force but you work with a much nicer class of person in this place.' He nodded at my two contacts and gave a large wink. 'Now, I guess you want the footage of Ms Mason arriving for her interview.' He fiddled with the controls of the player, and a picture came up of Philip Dow escorting a woman through a door. He froze the picture at that stage and looked at Philip.

Philip said: 'I can testify that that is Rosemary Mason in the picture. Her blouse is not the same as the one that was found in the drain at the hospital, but it's certainly possible that the slacks are the same.'

Ms Guchez looked at me, then added: 'I'd agree with those comments, but I'd also say that there are lots of slacks like that around, so while it's possible that they're the same I don't think a court would take it as hard evidence.'

'You're right, I'd have to agree, but it is one tiny step further forward. At least it doesn't take the clothing out of the picture completely as belonging to Ms Mason.'

We watched for a little while longer, as the interview started. There wasn't any sound, which was a pity as I'd have been interested to hear what Ms Mason sounded like, and also how Philip Dow was as an interviewer.

I actually found it a bit creepy watching a person who was now dead, and Philip Dow must have felt the same because he said:

'Not very nice, is it, watching someone who was murdered soon afterwards?'

'Just what I was thinking. I don't think there's much point

in watching more – the ID backup's really all we can get out of that.'

Ms Guchez didn't say anything, but she did look a bit paler than usual.

I turned to Bill.

'Thanks for your help, Bill. Good to know you're still some slight use to the community.'

He grinned. 'Always glad to help the fuzz, you know that. Now about the fee for this consultation….'

I snorted. 'Some habits you haven't lost then! A pint at the Red Bull, or wherever you uni blokes drink – that do you then?'

'Jeez, as mean as ever. I suppose it'll do on this occasion. Anyway, good to see you again, Len. If you ever think of moving to a decent job, just let me know. We may have something here.'

I snorted again. 'God, I hope I'm never that desperate…'

I went outside with the other two.

Philip started saying: 'I hope he wasn't too rude there.'

I laughed and said: 'We're old mates from way back. If I'd been too polite he'd have thought I'd gone off him…'

PHILIP

I was really pleased at the thought that Christiane would be around over Christmas – also that it wouldn't be yet another solo one for me, which I'd always found most depressing. In honour of the occasion I wanted to make it a real Christmas, so I went out for a bit of shopping. I found some quite nice Christmas decorations in one of the stationers – lengths of paper to make paper chains, balls and tinsel for Christmas trees, and things like that – and I also bought a box of Christmas crackers. I took all these home and tucked them away in my bedroom – then went out to the market to buy a Christmas tree. Most of the trees were rather large for our place, but I finally found one that was of the right size and wasn't too squashed or tired looking.

I kept the tree in the boot of my car, hoping that Christiane would go out for a long enough period. My luck was in when she was called in to the university because of a malfunction in the main computer system.

I got the tree out of the car and put it in a bucket with some sand that I'd filched earlier from a building site at the university.

I set it up in a corner of the front room, and decorated it with as many of the balls and tinsel streamers as I could – then cut it all back a bit because it was rather over the top. It was obvious I hadn't done that sort of thing for years.

Then I began to assemble several paper chains from the piles of paper slips, and I was quite pleased with the final results. I went and got a stepladder from the cellar, and stuck them to the front room cornices so that they streamed across the room. It looked quite festive if I say it myself, and I felt a bit like an excited kid at the end.

The best reward came when Christiane got home again. She went into the front room, and suddenly I heard a loud exclamation. She came out and into the kitchen where I was making coffee.

'It must be Christmas or something. I'm definitely staying now – I'd never get anything like this at home!'

'Thank you. I just wanted to have a real Christmas for one more time in my life.'

'Gosh, I hope you'll have a few more than this. You don't exactly look terminal yet.'

'True, but it's all just right this year and I wanted to make it a proper one.'

'I think you've certainly done that, and I'll allow you to make me a coffee to celebrate it.'

Which I did, with a small glow of contentment.

A PERSON AS YET UNNAMED

It's a bugger that the police have now found out that Rosemary Mason was originally Rhonda Miller. That means there's a chance that they could connect her to the hospital, though it was never a very long connection. However, my cousin works in the office at the police headquarters, and she's told me that they reckon it was one of the low-lifes who threatened Rhonda after her trial, and they're chasing all of them up. And even if they start thinking about here, I shouldn't be anywhere in the frame. They'll start thinking about the loonies, not me.

I've kept pretty quiet since that night, but I'm feeling the need for a bit more fun now and I think the time's ripe again. They haven't been chasing me yet and I don't think they will, so I'll start working on another campaign.

Now I'm looking for another good-looking young female who'll come across. And this time it's going to be one who won't be threatening me with exposure.

PHILIP

Christmas Day came and I started cooking early. I was a bit less confident now that I'd be able to pull all this off, but I'd written out a detailed timetable and I was trying to follow it. Christiane reckoned she hadn't cooked an English bread sauce before, and the French would never make such an atrocity, so I'd dug a recipe out for her.

And in the end it went surprisingly well. I'd baked the mince pies two days before, and a sample with yesterday's coffee had shown they were quite good. The chicken and potatoes this morning had roasted to a good golden brown, and the bread sauce when it was served was better than any I'd ever had before. Somehow that didn't totally surprise me.

I'd picked a nice bottle of wine, but as we were about to sit down Christiane produced a bottle and said: 'This is my contribution to the dinner.'

I couldn't believe my eyes – a bottle of Chateau Mouton Rothschild. I've seen them in really posh wine shops, but never in my life thought I might get to drink one.

'This is incredibly generous of you, but do you really want to open it now?'

'I most certainly do. And before you begin to speculate again about my sex life, yes it was given to me by a male who was trying to seduce me, and no he didn't achieve his goal, but once you've given a gift you don't get it back. I've been storing it very carefully so I hope it's still drinkable, and I've been keeping it for a special occasion. You're making this a special dinner – *et voilà*.'

The wine was exquisite, and I don't think I will ever forget the bouquet and rounded perfection of it. The meal wasn't quite of the same standard but it wasn't bad - especially the bread sauce...

During the meal I put on a recording of carols, and when it came to one in particular I said: 'You'll just have to let me pause for a moment for this one to sink in.' The music started softly, with those beautiful and evocative words:

Silent night, holy night;
All is calm, all is bright.
Round yon virgin, mother and child;
Holy Infant so tender and mild.

When the whole carol was sung I said: 'Thank you for that. That's the carol that most brings back to me the joys of Christmas as a small boy. After the rush and bustle up to Christmas it all becomes silent and peaceful, the frost outside's calm and bright, and those words tug at the heartstrings in a way that no other carol can do. It just brings back peace and serenity and happiness.'

'It strikes a real chord with me too.'

At the end of the meal Christiane said: 'That was delicious, and a lovely way to usher Christmas in. But you look a little sad…?'

'I was thinking that no matter how hard you try to recreate the magic that Christmas was to a small child, it just isn't the same when you're an adult. When I was little, life was rather mundane for most of the year, but as Christmas came on a magical world gradually seemed to open up – and "Silent Night" was one of the most magical parts of it. It took me into a whole different and peaceful world, away from every day cares.

'And I remember the anticipation for days wondering what presents might be coming, and whether there'd be anything in the stockings. And above all the feeling of being part of a family that's together, which didn't happen all that much in the rest of the year. There was just a magic that didn't come at any other time, but you can't recreate it. And as I think I told you once before, I was only twelve when it all ended.'

'How did your mother die?' She said it nicely, which took the sting out of it.

'It actually happened at Christmas, on Boxing Day. My mother was killed in a car crash.'

Christiane put her hand to her mouth.

'That wasn't the worst of it. There was an inquest, and suggestions were aired that my mother might have killed herself deliberately. She failed to take a bend and the car ran off the road into a tree, but she'd driven that road a hundred times before, and she wasn't drunk or anything. My parents had been having a tough time before that, but I've always tried to believe it was an accident because otherwise it would have been our faults. But my sister, who was seventeen at the time, believed with a vengeance that we were responsible, and she cut herself off from me and my father. We've haven't seen her again since that day.'

Christiane looked at me for a long minute; then she said: 'It wouldn't be adequate for me to offer my sympathy, though you certainly have it. If I can say one thing it's that I've also had my share of pain as I told you, and I'm firmly of the belief that one shouldn't dwell on the past. It's happened, be sad about it, but then move on and think of the positive things of life as well as the negative ones. And remember to be grateful for those positives.'

I reached out and put my hand on hers. 'Thank you – that's the nicest thought that anyone's given me for a long time. And thank you too for this dinner and the good company. A positive for which I'm truly grateful. I actually feel as though I've had something as good as a family Christmas – good company.' I grinned and added: 'I particularly enjoyed the wine. Especially knowing the circumstances of its provenance.'

Christiane put her tongue out at me, then said: 'I think we should continue to live in the present, and enjoy the positives. And I think we should let the wine achieve its intended goal. I think you should take me upstairs – right now....'

CHRISTIANE

Lying in bed later – alone – that night I couldn't help thinking about Philip losing his mother in the way that he did. It must have been one of the worst timings, when he was just changing from a child to a young adult. He'd already said that his father had little time for him, and he obviously wasn't much of a real parent. In contrast, he'd often spoken about his mother who he'd clearly been very fond of.

And that turned a key for me in understanding why Philip was probably like he was. Without his mother's influence he didn't develop the skills to interact with other people. He comes across as dull and boring when it's really that he just doesn't show his real self. He doesn't seem to know how to. It took me living in the same house to realise that there is a real human inside there. I just hope he can be persuaded to come out of that shell and live life fully. He's already been showing some signs of it – I'll try to keep it going.

The Asian girlfriend Lucy that he spoke about seems to have been an odd character herself, though she was an over-strong character rather than introverted. Still, two odds can sometimes hit it off well, and it seems that they did.

However, he's going to have to stop wishing that Christmas was still like he remembers it as a child, and things like that. You have to grow up and move on. Memories, yes, but then do it in a more adult way. Though we didn't do too badly today.

I do get the impression that just having me around in the same house has brought him out a bit. He just needs to keep it up.

SERGEANT NIELSEN

Christmas is over and I've managed to locate one more of my potential murder names – Raymond Ackerley. Brian Hawkins was proving good on these interviews, so I lined him up again and briefed him.

'This one's a bit different from the others. He's not as crudely violent as most of them are, but he's potentially just as nasty. He's a professional pornographer. That tells you something about his view of women. He was noted as attending every day of the trial and making notes, though in his case we have no idea what he would have been writing.

'He mostly produces videos of men with large pricks forcing themselves on to women who're initially reluctant, but then come across once they realise how exciting it all is. For the fantasies of inadequate men. He also puts out a range of stills of men who are very well endowed, with or without women hanging all over them. He's tried one or two videos of lesbian relationships, but I don't think they're his style. I don't know whether he's done any with gay men or not – he may have, and I'd guess again concentrating on the well-endowed ones.

'Most of his stuff that anyone knows about falls just within the R18 classification, though a lot of it's really pushing it, and he's had a number of prosecutions for selling stuff that isn't classified. And I'm sure they were only the tip of a large iceberg – a lot of his stuff goes out through the web, beneath any radar, and well into the classification of obscene.

'He's also been prosecuted for exploitation of women, and a certain amount of violence against them. However, his lawyer argued that in each case it was a misunderstanding, and somehow he got away with it. He did get one conviction for sex with an underage girl. He argued that she'd lied about her age, which she may well have – she was apparently keen to become that sort of actress, God knows why – but of course that isn't a defence and he was pinged.

'Not surprisingly, he doesn't want us anywhere near his premises, at least without a search warrant, so he was very happy to come in here.'

'Sounds lovely, Sarge. Do you want to do him or me?'

'You can have first go at him. I'd like to watch him – in particular his body language. He may well have nothing to do with Rosemary Mason, but I'd like to know a bit more about anyone of that type who's operating in our patch. Though I'm still a bit puzzled about why a pornographer would be so interested in a straight murder trial. Violence isn't one of his main themes, and it just doesn't sound like the sort of thing that would interest him all that much.'

When he arrived at the station he cut quite a different figure from the others we'd interviewed. He was dressed in a well-cut suit, with a pale pink open-necked shirt, and – ugh – a cravat. I know for a fact that he came from one of the poorer areas of

Lancaster, so I suppose he was trying to reinvent his image as the prosperous business man. His hair was well-dressed, if you like rather slicked back styles – which I don't.

Brian kicked the interview off with the standard introduction.

'Sir, we're investigating the murder of someone known as Rosemary Mason, who you would have known under her earlier name of Rhonda Miller because you attended her trial for killing her husband. We're interviewing all the people who attended the trial and showed a particular interest, in case they made further contact with her later. You did attend the trial quite regularly – would you like to comment on your interest in it? Did you in fact know Ms Miller before her trial?'

'Ah yes, I remember the trial because it was an unusual and interesting one. But no, I didn't know Ms Miller before the trial, and I wouldn't say I "knew" her at any stage – I just attended her trial.

'You may know that I'm a producer of art films, and I was interested in that trial in case I could have used it as a scenario for one of my films – something a bit different. That's why I took a lot of notes in the course of the trial. However, sadly it didn't work out as suitable, and I gave up the idea.'

It's a fair while since I've heard as much bollocks as that. I had to chip in.

'Sir, I don't recall any relevance of that trial to big pricks, which I know is your speciality.'

'Oh officer, you do me an injustice. Yes, some of my films may cater to certain male fantasies, but I have a much wider range of artistic interests than that.'

The injured innocence was rather spoiled by the smug expression that went with it. He knew he was bull-shitting us, and that we'd have trouble proving it.

'Sir, I have to ask you the same question that we've put to all the people we've interviewed. Where were you on the night of the tenth of June last?'

'Oh, I can't tell you that off the top of my head. You'll realise that I'm a very busy man at any time – far too many things to remember them all. But I keep a very detailed diary of all my engagements and activities – I can check that for you and get back to you.'

'Thank you, sir. To save you any extra trouble, PC Hawkins or I would be happy to come back with you to your office while you check the details.'

We got a very sharp look for that one. 'That won't be necessary, officer. I'm going back now, and as it happens I've got to be back in town in about an hour. If it's convenient for you I could drop in then with the details?'

More bullshit. He just didn't want us anywhere near his place, especially inside it. But we had no grounds on which to knock back his offer.

'Thank you, sir – we'd appreciate that. We'll see you a bit later this afternoon.'

When he'd gone I said to Brian: 'That's a slimy bullshitter if I've ever heard one. He ought to learn to smirk a bit less, though – it spoils the effect.'

'You're right there, Sarge. But do you reckon him in the frame for this one?'

'Probably not because it doesn't seem like his normal sort of thing to do, but I'm still puzzled as to why he'd pay so much attention to the trial. What he said was absolute crap, or course, but I just can't see what could have been in it for him.'

When Ackerley came back he was holding his diary, which was one of those with two days to an opening. He opened it to show the tenth of June.

'As you can see I had a hectic day's schedule filming "The Satyr and his Playmates". We started early and didn't finish until six o'clock. After that I would have had to look over the material that we shot, which would take me another couple of hours or so. After that I probably did my usual and ate at the Alhambra café, and then came home for a drink or two. Then bed for some sleep before the next day, which you can see had more filming.'

'Would anyone be able to corroborate that you were home and sleeping that night? It was the night time that we're particularly interested in.'

'I'm sorry, officer, but I live alone. I do sometimes have a playmate in, but not usually when I have such a busy schedule. I usually put a name on the page if anybody does stay, and there's nobody down for the tenth.'

'Thank you, sir – we'll be in touch if we need to ask you anything more.'

'My pleasure. Goodbye to you, and please say goodbye to the police constable as well.'

God, the bullshit never stops.

CHRISTIANE

Philip stopped me in the hallway this morning and said: 'You know you said the other day that you'd be prepared to look at what I've been trying to write. Well, I wondered if I could take you up on the offer? The condition would be that you don't have to say anything if you don't want to, and if you do say anything you must please be honest. Meaning if it's awful you can tell me so!'

Well, I'd made the offer so I have to stick by it now. And I guess I'm a bit interested to see what his writing's like.

'I did say that and I'm happy to do it. Under the conditions that you've just said. Do you have a printed copy or what?'

'I've printed a chunk out for you. I haven't written all that much yet. There's a bit more than I've printed out, but what I've printed'll give you a good enough idea of what it is. I'll just go and get it.'

He disappeared for a moment, and then returned with a handful of paper – mercifully not all that much by the look of it.

'This is it. It might be best if you take it away and read it in your own nest in the sky…'

I'd already decided that I'd do it privately, so I just thanked him and took it upstairs for some time later.

SERGEANT NIELSEN

One bit of serendipity – Albert Jones, who was on our list to interview in relation to Rosemary Mason's murder, was arrested for public drunkenness. I checked with the station sergeant who said that Jones would probably need to dry out a bit before anyone interviewed him.

Later in the day the sergeant told me he was probably okay now, so we hauled him up from the holding cell to the interview room.

'Right, Mr Jones, you've been arrested on a charge of public drunkenness, but that's not what we've got you up here for at the moment. You may remember a while ago that you attended the trial of a Rhonda Miller who'd been accused of murdering her husband. Rhonda Miller, who subsequently changed her name to Rosemary Mason, was herself murdered a few weeks ago, and we're speaking with all the people who were at that trial in case any of them had a grudge against her and killed her. This includes you.'

Jones didn't look like he'd remember much in life, but we had to ask. He sat for a moment, and then a cunning expression came over his face.

''Ere, what's in it for me, then?'

There was only one way to deal with this sort of response.

'Well, if you refuse to answer questions we'll assume you did it and we'll bang you up for that one as well as the drunkenness charge. If you admit it and you did actually do it, we'll arrest you for it but the judge'll probably go easier on you for the drunkenness. And if you admit it and you didn't do it we'll have you for wasting police time. What's it to be?'

I could see cogs slowly turning in his head.

'Yer, all right, ask me what you want to.'

'Do you remember going to Rhonda Miller's trial?'

'Yer, I think so. She was the bitch that done her 'usband in, right?'

'She was, but she'd been beaten up by her husband regularly, and the judge ruled that it was self-defence.'

'Self defence, my fucken' foot. Women shouldn't be allowed to do such things to their husbands. They should do what they're told to and not carry on.'

'Well, you should know that there are limits to that sort of thing, because you've been convicted in the past for beating up your wife, not to mention other public violence.'

'Yer, well, they was all mistakes. I didn't do it like they said, but the bitches made up stories and the judge believed them not me.'

'That was probably because there were witnesses who gave evidence in court as to what happened.'

'They was all women too. It's a conspiracy against us men. Who knows when it'll stop?'

'So did you kill Rhonda Miller, sir?'

'No I never done it and she can't say that I did. I only went to that trial because I had nowhere to go and the courthouse was cooler than outside.'

'Where were you on the night of June the tenth last?'

'Cor, I dunno. Where I always am of an evening, I guess – down the pub.'

'And what time would you have left the pub?'

'I dunno that either. I usually leave about half ten – sometimes a bit later.'

'Yes, well Ms Mason was killed at about half past eleven or later.'

'Well, couldn't have been me then. I'm always in bed by then. If I can find me way there. Anyway, you want to know when I left the pub – they have them camera things in the pubs now. You could check it and see when I went.'

No chance that the footage would still exist now, but he was probably only trying to be helpful. 'Which pub would that have been, sir – the Fox and Grapes?'

'Yer, that's me usual.'

'Right, sir, thank you for your assistance. Constable Hawkins'll show you back to your cell, then.'

''Ere, what do I get for helping you lot then? You going to release me on this charge then? I never did no harm anyway.'

'That'll be up to the charging officer.'

And he was escorted out.

Hawkins came back after he'd delivered him back to the cells.

'So what do you make of that, Sarge? Do you think he could have done it?'

'I think just about all the other suspects are more likely than him. He's not a very pleasant man, but I can't see him doing that sort of thing. It would have been too premeditated. I don't think he does premeditated any more – there's not enough brain cells left.'

CHRISTIANE: PHILIP'S STORY

Philip's gone away for the day, and with him out of the way it seems a good time to look at the story that he'd given me. There'd be no pressure on me to comment immediately, and I knew I'd have to be careful in what I said and how I said it.

It had no title at this stage. And when I read it, the story was completely unexpected. It proved to be very much like an old-fashioned fairy tale, like the ones I'd read when I was little, but there was probably a more modern point behind it. And maybe some clues to Philip's own life.

Part of what he'd given me ran like this:

> A woodcutter and his wife had one child, a son Peter. They lived deep in a forest with no other people nearby, and although they had a happy and comfortable life Peter often wished that he had a brother or sister to play with, or even a few neighbouring children.
>
> One day Peter's mother took him aside and said: 'Peter, it is time for you to leave on a quest, to find the one with whom you will spend the rest of your life.'

Peter asked: 'How will I know where to go? And who will help me for I do not have enough experience of the world to manage such a journey?'

His mother said: 'These two creatures will travel with you and will help you as you need. This is Knutley' – she pointed at a fluffy red squirrel – and then she indicated a pinkish-brown bird with beautiful bright blue flashes on its wings – 'and this is a jay, and her name is Kay.'

Peter looked at these creatures in amazement – how were they ever going to help him on a long and unknown journey?

'Mother, it is kind of you to give me these creatures to help, but are you sure they will know what to do?'

His mother looked at him. 'Have faith and you will find out. And now I will give you two other things to help you on your journey. Take this small loaf of bread which will give you a start, and this box of matches, and put them in your satchel. You will not be able to carry more than that, but it should be enough.'

Peter looked in alarm at the small size of the loaf of bread – it was little more than a bread roll – but he knew that his mother was very wise and he felt that he had to trust her. So he set out, accompanied by the squirrel and the jay. They walked down the long path that led from their house, which Peter's father had told him led to the main towns. Every now and then Peter took a bite from the bread roll, and it wasn't long before there was little left of that. At that he began to feel worried, and also a bit lonely.

He sighed loudly. 'I wish there was someone to talk to,

that I could share my thoughts and worries with.'

'Well, there's always us,' said Knutley.

Peter stared at the squirrel in astonishment. 'But people and squirrels can't talk to each other, can they?!'

'Well, we are, aren't we? Of course they can – it's just that no humans ever try.' He sounded a little disdainful.

'That's right,' said Kay. 'We've often wondered what it would be like to talk to a human, but they don't give us the chance.'

So when Peter got used to the idea he said: 'Well, I'm worried that I've almost run out of food and I've hardly started my journey.'

Knutley looked at him in astonishment. 'Well, there's plenty of food around here – you just have to collect it.'

Peter looked around, and could see nothing. 'But I don't know what to do,' he said in despair.

Knutley looked unimpressed. 'Well, we'll just have to show you,' he said. 'Sit down on this bank for a while, and we'll bring it to you.'

So Peter sat down, and because he was tired he soon fell asleep. He was woken again by the pattering of many tiny feet, and lots of excited squeaking. He looked up and saw a whole tribe of squirrels, each carrying some food. Many had little piles of nuts, of at least seven different sorts. Others had tiny fruits from the forest. And a few were carrying little mushrooms and fungi, of types that Peter had never seen before.

'These are my cousins,' said Knutley. 'I got them to help me so that there's plenty of food, and I thought we could then all sit down and talk together. I haven't seen some of these cousins for several years.'

He began to organise them to sort the food into separate piles. As he did that, Kay flew back into the clearing with some pieces of fresh meat in her beak. She spoke to Peter.

'These squirrels only ever eat bits of plants, so I've brought you some real food. I eat insects, birds' eggs and little animals, but I thought you might not like those so I've brought you some fresh meat. I can eat it raw as it is now, but I thought you might prefer to light a small fire and cook yours.'

'And you might also like to cook one or two of the mushrooms,' said Knutley. 'I've heard that humans can't eat all of them when they're not cooked – it does funny things to their insides.'

So Peter collected some sticks and used one of his mother's matches to light a small fire. He cooked his food, and he sat with Kay and all the squirrels and they ate together contentedly. Somehow Peter felt less lonely then, even though there were no other people around.

As they munched Peter turned to Kay and said: 'I can see that the squirrels could find all the nuts and fruits in the forest because they know where they are, but how did you find the fresh meat?'

'Well,' said Kay. 'there's a small village some way from here, and I found some meat that had just been put out for one of the dogs there. He had plenty, so I just helped myself to a few pieces.'

'Did the dog not mind that?'

'Well, he didn't actually see me,' replied Kay.

'But that's stealing then, isn't it, and my mother always told me that that's wrong.'

'Well, yes, I suppose it is. But the dog had plenty of food and I thought that you needed it more. My cousin the jackdaw taught me how to steal things and not get caught – he's famous around the world as a thief.'

So Peter ate the food with the other creatures, and then he packed some of what was left in his satchel. The squirrels took the rest of the food, especially the nuts which they said they would store in their larders.

In the morning they all said their goodbyes, and then Peter, Knutley and Kay set off again down the long track.

Peter ate the occasional nut from his pack for energy as he went, but after a while he said: 'I'm really sorry that I don't have any of my mother's bread left. It would have gone so well with the other food.'

There was silence for a moment, and then Kay said: 'There's a village not far from here and I've heard that there's a champion baker there. You could buy some bread from her.'

'But I have no money,' said Peter.

'No problem,' said Kay. 'I will find you something that you can barter with.'

She flew away, and in a while she came back with a gold ring in her beak. Peter looked at it, and said: 'I think you've been stealing again. I couldn't possibly use this – the baker would know that it's not mine.'

'Well, put it in your pocket then. I can't return it now to where it came from, and you may yet find a use for it one day. I'll go and look for something else.'

The next time she came back with a small nugget of gold in her beak.

'I haven't stolen this. There is a rocky area to the west of the forest where these are just lying on the ground, and I know that the humans prize these very highly.'

So they made their way to the village, and Peter found the baker and was able to exchange his nugget for two quite large loaves of bread. The baker said: 'Where did you find such a beautiful nugget of gold?', but Peter replied that it was somewhere in the forest and he couldn't remember how to get back to it now. The baker looked suspiciously at him, but she couldn't say any more.

And when they stopped for lunch they found that the bread was indeed delicious. Kay didn't partake of it but went to find herself more meat, but Knutley did eat a small piece. However, he said that it didn't have the flavour of the forest nuts and fruits and he went back to those.

That's enough to give you an idea of the writing. It went on for some time with various other happenings and escapades of the threesome, but it was unfinished as Philip had told me. My guess would be that in the story Peter will eventually find a beautiful young girl, to whom he will propose with the ring that Kay had thoughtfully given to him early in the tale.

Well, it is a fairy story after all.

And after all that I didn't quite know what to make of it. I'd have to say that his writing style was good – simple, clear and effective, and it flowed well. Imagination? Well, it was good though perhaps a bit derivative from many traditional fairy tales, but that said there were some nice new touches as well, including a gentle sense of humour. I did like Knutley's slightly sharp sense of humour.

Publishability? Not being a writer myself I have no idea, but I'm not sure that this is the sort of thing that any publisher would want these days, in fact I'd strongly doubt it. Then again you never know what might just appeal to someone. There have been well-publicised cases recently of authors who've had multiple rejections from everywhere, and then one publisher picks it up and it's a global success. On the other hand, I had a friend a while ago who wrote fiction, and had rejection after rejection from publishers which got her quite depressed in the end. I fear that Philip may have to face the same fate, though it would be nice if not.

And then the big question – did Philip have some personal motive in writing this particular story about a young man chasing happiness and a beautiful young woman. Peter is a child alone in a sense – there are some parallels, including that Peter feels himself to be a bit inadequate and inept. Shades of Philip in that as well?

But I don't think I'm going there....

CHRISTIANE

We were having one of our joint coffee sessions, which had become quite regular. No home-cooked biscuits this time – I don't think either of us had had time to bake any.

Philip seemed a bit preoccupied, so I asked him what was on his mind.

'I was thinking about differences between males and females. Not the obvious physical ones, but thoughts and attitudes. I've just been conducting several interviews for staff, of both genders, and the men have been depressingly predictable in what they think and what they say. Superiority of men, macho attitudes, fixed thoughts on everything. Women take your questions and think about them before they answer. Then they come out with a variety of responses, often quite imaginative, and usually sensible. I sometimes despair for my gender.'

'I wouldn't have put it quite that strongly, but I guess I don't interview as much as you do. I've only got a small unit that I have to staff. But I think I know broadly what you mean.'

'I could go on a bit more and say that in general conversation I find women usually much more rewarding to talk to. Again the men are predictable, and they mostly want to talk about themselves, anyway. The women have a much wider range of thoughts. You can't totally generalise, of course. There are women who're totally self-centred drama queens – everything's about them and their problems – and there are some who're plain bitchy. Also you do get some men who think more laterally than most. But women often surprise me with their range of responses to things, and they're often quite wise thoughts that they have. Interesting too. I've sometimes wondered whether it's because women also have such a range of situations that they have to cope with – they get more practice.'

'I know what you mean with that, but I think it's something a bit more innate than just being trained to cope. I've long thought that women's brains fire off in different directions from men's – which doesn't mean that either's in any way better – just that they're different.'

'I always find that if I'm sitting in the tearoom having a break and I start chatting to someone, if it's a male they'll half the time be trying to impress you with how wonderful they are over something they've done, or even worse they'll try to score points off you. Women'll talk about all sorts of things, and they're more likely to be interested in your views on the same things. Though I'd have to say that usually I'm just interested to hear what they have to say. As I said before, there's often a lot of wisdom there.'

'I agree with your general drift, but I think you're giving women a bit much credit there. And I'd also say it can be quite a bit different when it's women talking to other women. It can get quite bitchy and catty, with points being scored too. They just can't be bothered to do that with men, maybe. They know they're better than the men, whereas they have to compete with other women?!'

'In the spirit of competition and the war between the sexes, let's just call it a one-all draw...'

The coffee was finished and we went on our separate ways. Later in the day I thought again about the conversation, and I thought maybe I'd been a bit hard on Philip. I think he'd read the situation quite well – he was just giving more credit to women than perhaps we deserved overall. Interesting, though, that he enjoys talking to women, when I'd thought he didn't like much social contact at all. And not all that many men would have thought that way at all – certainly not a lot of the ones I've known.

AGGIE RANSOME

Aggie shuffled towards the kitchen, which was now empty. Lunch had been served and washed up, and the staff were gone until late afternoon. She knew her way intimately around the kitchen, with its huge cooking cauldrons, its industrial sized blenders and peelers and other processors. She went calmly over to the knife drawer, which should have been locked but not for the first time it wasn't.

She rummaged around in the drawer and selected a boning knife, with a thin blade. She felt the edge, and it was extremely sharp. She put it into the capacious pocket in the front of her apron, and shuffled out of the kitchen again.

She went slowly across the grounds until she came to Mansfield Ward. She wandered into the ward and started to empty the wastepaper baskets into a bag that she carried with her – one of her regular chores in various parts of the hospital. The charge nurse glanced up, saw it was only Aggie, and went back to filling in a patient report.

Aggie drifted in to the charge nurse's office and emptied his bin, then turned to go out. But standing behind him she quickly pulled out the knife and with a great yell she plunged it into his back with all her might. She pulled it out, then plunged it again, although the nurse was falling forward now. He screamed out in pain, and one of the ward patients came over to see what the fuss was about. The patient stared at the scene for a moment, then said 'Oh' and walked away again. None of the staff in neighbouring wards were close enough to hear.

Aggie pulled the knife back and drove it in yet again. 'That's for Uncle Bertie!' she shouted. 'You bastard!' Blood was welling everywhere, and she got a lot of it on her apron, but she didn't seem to care. Finally the charge nurse was moving no more, and she walked out of the ward, now in something of a daze. She came across the charge nurse from the next ward, and said 'I've killed Uncle Bertie.' She waved the bloodstained knife at him.

'Shit!' said the other charge nurse. 'You'd better show me.'

They went into Mansfield Ward and he saw the scene of carnage.

'Come back with me and sit in my ward, and we'll sort things out,' he said as calmly as he could. They went back to his office, and he sat Aggie down with a glass of water to distract her, then phoned the central switchboard and gave them a rather garbled account of what had happened. He thought of going to see if the other nurse could still use some first aid, but it hadn't looked like it and he couldn't really leave Aggie alone with his patients. She was still muttering about Uncle Bertie, though she seemed to have become somewhat calmer again.

Police and ambulance arrived very quickly, and found that the charge nurse was showing no signs of life. The police closed off the office pending the arrival of forensic officers, and Inspector Brady came to interview Aggie. This was not productive, because she refused to utter a word.

Aggie was taken back to her own ward, which then had to be locked until it could be determined what should be done with her, and the charge nurse from the adjacent ward was put in charge of both until the police investigation in the office had finished.

There was a sense of shock throughout the hospital – less because of the death of the charge nurse, and rather more because Aggie had been such a well-known and loved figure around the hospital for fifty years or so. You never can tell, said some, but rather more people felt that it probably wasn't just a patient suddenly becoming murderous out of the blue. There had to be something more behind it.

LANCASTER POLICE HQ

Back in the station there was an emergency meeting to discuss this latest crime. Inspector Brady spoke first.

'On the surface of it, a mental patient went feral and killed one of the charge nurses, and it may have been nothing more than that. We've recently been getting a little evidence that the murder of Rosemary Mason may have some connection with the Royal Vic Hospital, but Aggie Ransome couldn't in any way have been involved with that killing, so it's hard to see how there could be any link now. It'd be nice if we could talk to Aggie and try to find out what pushed her to do it, after what were apparently fifty peaceful years of living in the hospital, but I tried and she wouldn't say a word.'

Sergeant Nielsen did some quick thinking. It was probably not surprising that Inspector Brady's style of interrogating would have clammed Aggie up, but he thought that maybe he could make a gentler approach if he could get another chance to talk to her. But how to put this tactfully to Inspector Brady?

'Sir, it's always going to be hard to get someone like Aggie to open up, but I just have a thought. She was put in the hospital because she was interfered with by her uncle, and that's the sort of justice that happened when she was little. I had a niece who was also interfered with by a man – he wasn't a relative, I hasten to add, but I just thought that if I started off by saying that, and how I knew what it was like for a young girl, we might just find a bit of common ground and she might talk.'

Inspector Brady grunted, but after a moment said: 'Well, it might be worth a go. It shouldn't do any harm, anyway. How d'you propose to do this?'

'Sir, I think I should contact the hospital and ask for a small, pleasant and private room to be made available for me to talk to Aggie in. Normally I'd say that somebody else should also be present for the interview, but in this case I think quite strongly that it should be just me. I'll wear a concealed recorder which should be enough to use her comments as evidence, if I can get any out of her. Does that sound OK, sir?'

'Hm, yes, I suppose you can go ahead.'

He didn't sound enthusiastic, but Sergeant Nielsen was happy enough.

SERGEANT NIELSEN

I'd arranged for a comfortable sitting room in the hospital to be made available, and I'd said it was absolutely vital that we weren't disturbed once Aggie'd come to meet with me. This was going to take a lot of care, and I'd probably only get one shot at it.

Aggie came in with one of the charge nurses. He said: 'Here you are, Aggie – this is the bloke as wants to have a chat wi' yer.' And he left again.

'Eh oop, Aggie. Sit yerself down and make yerself comfortable.

'I had a young niece once who was interfered with by a friend of the family, and I know what a terrible thing that is for a young girl. I've tried to help her, but I can see that she'll never fully get over what happened to her. And I've heard that something like that happened to you too, with your Uncle Bertie. Would you like to tell me a bit more about it?'

I tried to keep my expression neutral, and I didn't stare at her but tried to show that I was still paying attention to her.

She gave me a very long stare, while I held my breath, and

then it worked.

'He was a horrible, horrible man. He pushed himself into our family, he did awful things to me, and he took away my freedom. They stuck me in here, and I've been here for the whole of my life. I used to pray to God that something awful would happen to Uncle Bertie, but I never heard that it did. I'm not sure I believe in God any more.'

'But you told the charge nurse from next door to Mansfield that you'd killed Uncle Bertie. Is that what you did?'

'Well, I hoped it was, but I think it was actually Mr Slater from Mansfield. But he was as bad as Uncle Bertie.'

'Oh aye, do you mean he also interfered with people that he shouldn't have?'

'Aye, he used to take some of his female patients into the little room at the back of the ward, and he did things to them on the bed. I used to see them through the little window when I was doing me rounds.'

'You didn't mention this to any of the other staff?'

'What good would that have done?' she said bitterly. 'Nobody believed me when I told them about Uncle Bertie or I wouldn't have been in here. Why would they believe what a patient says against the word of a nurse?'

There would have been a lot of truth in that. Then Aggie spoke again.

'The worst thing he ever did was when he killed that poor lassie – the one you found on the railway.'

That hit me with a sledgehammer. The first bit of concrete evidence that we've had, assuming it's true. More care needed to keep this going.

'I saw her on the night she died. I've never been able to sleep well since I came here, and I get up and wander around the hospital gardens. I like to watch the owls and listen to them. They're my friends, the owls.

'I was standing near the gate in the wall that evening, and she came in through the gate in the wall and walked towards the kitchens where you go into the main corridor. I saw it was Rosemary Mason – I knew her because she was one of them who was nice to me while she was in here. I never thought she should have been here either – she wasn't any sort of nutter.

'She didn't see me, and I didn't like to call out. She went into the building, and I guessed she was going to Mansfield. She was a patient in there – don't know why, because they're mostly pretty daft in there. Anyway, I always thought that she was one of the ones that Mr Slater did things with, so I went round to the little window and looked in. She wasn't there at first, but then I saw that she was on the bed and Mr Slater was doing those things to her. But when he'd finished she never got up. She just didn't move at all. That didn't look right. And it made my blood boil because he was just as bad as Uncle Bertie, and he deserved to die like Uncle Bertie.'

I was gobsmacked, but I had to try and act as though I'd just been told something quite normal.

'Aye, we were beginning to wonder about one of the nurses here because one of their cars was seen near where Rosemary's body was put on the railway line, but we weren't sure because he was supposed to be on duty here that night. He couldn't have gone out then, could he?'

'Oh aye, he wouldn't have had any trouble in the middle of the night. It's very quiet then – he could have easily gone out for half an hour or more.'

'Thank you, Aggie – you've helped me a great deal. I think you know a lot more about what goes on in here than anyone else. Certainly more than we did.'

'They're not going to let me out of here though, are they?'

I really felt for her then. I think she believed that she'd killed the demon who was keeping her in this imprisonment, but still nothing was going to change. Life certainly wasn't fair from her perspective.

'I'm sorry, but I think you're probably right, Aggie. Life just isn't fair, is it?'

What else could I say? Aggie got up to walk out. She didn't say anything more, but the expression on her face told it all.

CHRISTIANE

With all the hoo-ha over Aggie and the murder of the nurse at the Royal Victoria Hospital, I hadn't had the time or suitable opportunity to get back to Philip about his writing. I decided that I had to bite the bullet on that one now, but a good way to do it would be for me to cook my French variation on the shortbread of which he's so fond – sablés.

I'm not much of a cook of anything sweet – I mostly helped maman with savoury dishes when I was smaller. However, I'd helped with sablés once and I thought I could remember enough.

I dug out several recipes and looked them over. The nicest one seemed to have ground almond meal added, and a pinch of cinnamon which I love. Some of them were iced after cooking, but I don't remember ours at home having any icing so I passed on that one.

I got together the ingredients and made the mixture, which the recipe said should then be stood for twenty-four hours. I put it in the back of the fridge, and Philip didn't seem to notice it – at least if he did he didn't ask what it was.

Next morning I told Philip he had to come to morning tea for a treat, and then I baked the biscuits. A quick taste told me that they weren't too bad – not up to maman's standard but quite edible.

Philip rolled up for morning tea – he'd probably smelled the baking. I sat him down with coffee and a couple of the sablés, and explained about their tradition. Then I said:

'I still owe you some thoughts on your writing, but the business with Aggie and the hospital distracted me.'

'Well, I did say that you needn't feel obliged to say anything.'

'But I would like to, though it may not be adequate. I very much enjoyed reading it, and I was a little sad not to find out what happened to Peter in the end. The story certainly gets you in.

'You have a nicely simple style of writing, which is meant very much as praise – it isn't convoluted or fussy or anything. The storyline reminded me a lot of some fairy stories that I read when I was little, though in other ways it was different but I can't quite define how.

'I enjoyed the characters of Knutley and Kay, who I thought had an appropriate view of human foibles. With Peter, did I also detect a slight air of loneliness? Which if I'm going to be a bit impertinent I could say reminded me of you.'

'I think that's a fair comment about the loneliness, yes. How much it relates to me I can't really say. I guess any author puts something of themselves and their experience into what they write, but I can't say how much in my case. The fairy tale theme came to me because one of my happiest memories as a small child was my mother reading me fairy stories as I lay in bed. They were a great comfort even if some of the characters were a bit scary.' He grinned. 'I can say, however, that it doesn't all relate to my childhood – I've never met a talking squirrel or jay!'

'Mm, they weren't common in the Pyrenees when I was little, either. So I think the thing I'd like to say in summary is that I wanted to find out what happened in the end – not just what happened, but how it happened – all the events along the way. And if the reader wants that, the writer must be doing something right.'

'Thank you – that's all very kind, and much more positive than I was expecting. I wanted to do it just for personal satisfaction – to see if I could write anything at all – but I don't imagine that it'll go any further than that. I don't imagine that any publisher would be interested in it – too old fashioned.'

'Yes, sorry, that was the other aspect that I meant to add. Because I have no experience of writing I have absolutely no idea about its publishability. All I can say is from the reported experience of friends who've tried a bit of writing, which is that you get huge numbers of rejections, and occasionally an acceptance, with no rhyme or reason about it. Something can fail umpteen times, and then be accepted and be a major hit so somebody's judgment was a bit askew. But rejections, I'm afraid, are par for the course.'

'Thank you so much. I owe you for that – not just for the comments but for being prepared to make them at all. It can be hard to get involved in something that's very personal for the other person.

'And by the way – you bake a mean sablé. I think I'll have to stop baking my shortbread and cede the field to you.'

'Don't you dare! I only stay in this house because of your shortbreads… But if you agree to keep making them I'll try another of my mother's favourites some time. It's Kouign Amann, which is a very buttery creation between a cake and a pastry, and it's a Breton speciality. My mother was Breton – it's probably her genes that make me as contrary as I am.'

'You'll have to try harder if I'm going to see you as contrary. But with the kouign amann – you're definitely on. I'll look forward to it.'

LANCASTER POLICE HQ

The CID team met to consider Aggie Ransome's evidence and what could be done with it. As usual, Inspector Brady took the lead.

'I think we've probably got an answer as to who killed Rosemary Mason. If I recall right, one of the people who owned a white estate car was a nurse at a mental hospital, but he was discounted because he was on duty that night. But Aggie told Len that he'd have had no trouble sneaking out for enough time to dispose of the body. The spot where it was placed is pretty close to the hospital.

'I reckon our next job'll be to go over Mansfield Ward very carefully to see what if any evidence there may be of sexual activities – in particular in the small back room that Aggie spoke of. Len – could you get that organised with forensics, and have a look over yourself?

'Aye, I'll get straight on with that, sir.'

'And we're still faced with what now to do with Aggie Ransome. My recollection of the law is that anyone who's a committed patient in a mental institution can't be prosecuted for anything that they do while they're committed, though I'm not sure whether that applies to all offences. It's a bone of contention with some of the local traders in Lancaster. Some of the patients are allowed out, and they go and shoplift in newsagencies, supermarkets and so on because they know they can't be done for it. But whether it applies to something like murder I'm not sure – we'll have to get legal advice on that. Obviously Aggie can't be allowed out of the hospital, but it seems to me it's the decision of the hospital authorities what they do with her inside.

'Any further comments or questions?'

As usual there were none.

PHILIP

With the desperately sad news involving Aggie, I thought we needed something a bit different to take our minds off all the recent events. I'd found a salad that was a bit different from anything I'd done before.

I checked that Christiane was available because in one sense she was a focus for the experiment, and then went out to buy the ingredients. I bought a ready cooked chicken from a small Portuguese rotisserie in the market, because their chickens were infinitely more tasty than any I could cook, or any of the other fast chicken outlets. No comparison with those, certainly. Then I bought the salad ingredients. After I'd got them I thought they seemed a bit simple, but it was too late now.

We sat down and I served the chicken – then put the salad, which was in a nice white bowl, on the table. It was certainly colourful – hopefully also a bit more than just that.

'You're a bit of a guinea pig – I've never made this salad before. When you've finished I'd be interested in an unbiased assessment. It's a complete experiment – no offence taken if you don't like it. I mightn't like it either.'

Christiane served herself a reasonable portion, and then used her fork to investigate the ingredients. Her eyebrows lifted slightly, and she sampled a good forkful.

'Mm, this is very nice, but that's not the final verdict. Let me eat some more.'

We continued eating, and I was pleased that I also thought it wasn't too bad. Between us we managed to empty the bowl, which I thought had to be a good sign.

When we'd finished Christiane said: 'Philip, you continue to amaze me. That was really delicious, and I've never had a salad quite like it before. I think I can see what went into it, but how about you tell me in better detail?'

'It's awfully simple really – red cabbage, fresh pears and quite a few fresh coriander leaves, with some lemon juice, oil and salt and pepper to dress it. Nothing more than that. I was worried that it wasn't quite exciting enough, but I think in the end it all went together quite well.'

'It certainly did. So how exactly did you prepare it?'

'Well, I didn't follow the recipe to the letter. It said to coarsely chop all the main ingredients and then put them in a food processor for eight seconds, but I was worried that that would make it all a bit mushy. I prefer a bit of texture in a salad, so what I did was chop the red cabbage into strips as thinly as I could, and then do the pears a bit more roughly. Then I just tore the coriander leaves fairly coarsely because I love their flavour and I didn't want to lose that. For the red cabbage it would have been nice to have had one of those mandolin things that cooks use to get really thin slices, but I don't have one of them.'

'Well, I think it was perfect like that. I totally agree with you about texture, and the flavours went together beautifully.

But where did all this come from? You've never ventured into anything quite as novel as this before.'

'It was you being here, actually.' I could feel myself going pink, but I couldn't help it. 'I really enjoy nice food, but doing anything like that for one person's a complete waste of time in my view. The enjoyment of food's ten per cent the taste of the food and ninety per cent the pleasure of sharing it with someone else. At least as long as they enjoy it too!'

'I don't quite know what to say. I'm getting embarrassed now as well. I can only say that I'm glad I'm not just an intrusion in this house.'

'I hope you said that last bit tongue in cheek. You know perfectly well that you aren't any sort of intrusion, and I'm hoping and thinking that you now find this place a home rather than just a lodging. The other day you referred to the now flourishing rosemary bush in the yard as "our" herbs, which pleased me hugely. And I think the rosemary must enjoy having you here as much as I do, or it wouldn't be growing like it is!'

'I'd like to add one more thing. As much as I enjoyed the taste of the salad I also loved being transported back to my childhood and my mother's wonderful cooking. She used to use fresh coriander a lot in her dishes, and I absolutely adored it, but it isn't used nearly enough by people in England and I haven't had any for ages. So thank you too for that lovely memory. And now I think I need a refill of wine, please, or I'll go weepy...'

SERGEANT NIELSEN

I thought I'd better get on with the inspection of Mansfield Ward as soon as possible, so I called my mate Frank Elliott and asked him if he could accompany me. I thought it'd help me to have someone who knew all about the hospital's workings, and it wasn't likely that there'd be any contamination of evidence.

I called him and fixed for the same afternoon. He reckoned the rats and blackclocks could wait for another day. His friendly smile was very welcome – this hospital always gives me the spooks a bit.

'How do, Len. A' reet?'

'Aye, not so bad, thanks. At least we've been getting somewhere now with this murder, even if we did have to get Aggie's help to do it.'

'Aye, we did. I tried once before when Christina and her friend Philip were here, but she weren't going to talk with them there. A pity I couldn't get it out then – it would have saved a lot of unpleasantness.'

'Aye, it would have, but it's not your fault. Anyway, can we go and have a look at Mansfield Ward?'

Frank led the way, greeting patients all the way. He seemed to be well regarded by most of them. One of them came up to me and tried to give me his badge of one of the football clubs, but Frank said "Nay, don't give him that one – that isn't his team. That one's yours". Afterwards he said to me: "He'd have been real upset if you'd taken it – it's probably his prize possession".

We got to the door, which was closed off by crime scene tape – he said the patients had been spread out temporarily to other wards. I broke the tape and we went in.

The first thing that struck me was the smell – a sort of old and rank smell of various unpleasant things.

'Phew, it's not the freshest in here, is it?'

'Aye, but yer get used to it in time. This is nowhere near the worst, I can tell you.'

'Hm. So just give me a run-down on the layout, could you?'

'Well, this is obviously the main part of the ward where the patients spend their time. They'd mostly be sitting in these chairs around the edge, and in this ward where they don't have much of a mental age they probably spend most of their days in the chairs. A few might play a game at the table over there. And those are their beds – one locker each for their things.

'Then that's the charge nurse's office over there, where Mr Slater was most of the time. At the back there are toilets and bathing facilities, and then there's that small room over there, which has a couple of beds in it. It's not used most of the time, but it's there in case a patient needs to be kept apart from the others for any reason.'

'Aye, well that's where Aggie said he did his business with the females. I'll have to have a good look through the office while I'm here, but we might do that back room first if we could.'

We went into the room, which was pretty plain and spartan. The two beds were made up with dark and thin blankets on the top. On one of the blankets I noticed several fairly broad, dark stains which looked very like blood stains.

I said to Frank: 'I don't know if you'd heard, but there were some quite deep cuts on Rosemary Mason's right arm. These stains are in the right position to have been from her arm if she'd been lying on her back. I'd like to take this with me for DNA testing – it could clinch the evidence finally if it's her blood. I've got an evidence bag with me.'

We took the blanket off, folded it neatly and I put it in the bag. I poked around the rest of the room, including under the mattress, but I didn't find anything else. Then I went to the office and searched the desk and filing cabinet. Most of the stuff was hospital forms and reports. There were a couple of pretty iffy porn magazines, but you'd probably find that in some of the other ward offices too. Sitting there in that atmosphere day after day can't have been very exciting.

That done I said: 'I can't see much point in going through all the patients' cupboards – he'd hardly have kept anything there.'

'Aye, mostly you'd find blackclocks and ants. If I'd been a bit quicker off the mark I'd have brought a sprayer with me and got you to do some of me work for me.'

'Mebbe I should just poke around behind the lockers and cupboards, though, in case he'd dropped the knife there. We've never found that.'

I started going along one wall, behind every bed locker, and then down the other side. Suddenly I got the shock of my life.

'Jesus, Frank, I think there's a body here!'

I pointed to where a foot with a black shoe on it was pro-truding from under one of the beds.

Frank came over and said "Huh?". Then he turned to me and grinned. He took hold of the shoe and pulled. Out came a whole leg, and nothing else, but by that stage even I could see from the too-bright pinkness that it was a prosthetic limb, and not real.

'Jesus, you might have warned me!'

'Aye, I didn't think of it. I know what it's like – it took me the same way when it first happened to me. It must be old Charlie's – he didn't get to tek it wi' him when he were moved to t'other ward. He's quite used to hopping and I don't think the leg fits him all that well anyway.'

When I'd finished he had to lead me out of the hospital because I'd completely lost my sense of direction getting to the ward. Then I headed off back to the station to get the blanket stains analysed.

CHRISTIANE

I was sitting with Philip having a cup of coffee – sans biscuits this time. With the shock of the murder of the nurse at the hospital and the realisation of what Aggie's life had been like, I don't think either of us felt like baking. Even though we were very marginal to all the happenings, it still felt as though we'd been part of it.

I said to Philip: 'I'm forever amazed at how little progress the human species has made over the centuries in treating all people as equal. When I think of how Aggie was condemned to an institution with a life sentence for nothing more than being an attractive girl when a man wanted to have his way with her. And the nurse must have had some hold over Rosemary Mason. Maybe he threatened to expose her if she didn't cooperate. It just makes me sick. And I can quote a number of my friends – female – who've also had things done to them because the men had some sort of power over them. You may think differently as a male, but it horrifies me.'

Philip was silent for a moment; then he said: 'I think just

the same as you, actually. I've also known women who've been mistreated by men. One of the earliest girls I was keen on was the first of them. We were talking about how we each lost our virginity, and she said "Mine was on my first date with a guy who wouldn't take no for an answer". It didn't strike me instantly, until a bit later when I realised it meant she'd been date-raped, and I was horrified.'

'I've certainly known too many women who've had sex forced on them one way or another. And the attitude of so many males – "oh, she was asking for it" when she didn't say a word except maybe no. In my book if a girl is asking for it, she says so in clear words. You don't make an assumption because you think that her skirt's a bit short and that's sending you a signal.'

'I hope you never had that sort of experience yourself – a sexual attack, I mean, not the domestic violence from Giampaolo?'

'I did have a very hard word put on me a couple of times. On the one occasion I shouted out really firmly and loudly that he had to stop immediately or there'd be consequences, and he did stop. I think he was surprised because he thought I'd be a pushover. If I'd have had to follow through with the consequences I'm not sure I'd have known what to do, but fortunately I didn't have to.

'On the second occasion it was far more serious – I was grabbed and the offender – who I knew, incidentally – started trying to strip my clothes off. I was really furious that time, and rage took over. I appeared to relax for a moment, and he relaxed too, probably thinking I was coming across. At which moment I kneed him very hard in the balls. Really hard. He started screaming in agony. He also yelled abuse at me and threatened all sorts of reprisals, but he was in too much pain to be able to do much. He did try to grab me but I don't think he could see too clearly. I slapped him really hard across the face, enough to jolt his head sideways, and walked out of his room. What then pleased me even more than his screaming was the fact that this happened in his room in a university residence. I left the door open as I went, and people passing in the corridor started looking at the commotion. I said to them "that's what happens when you try to rape someone" and walked off. It should at least have been a talking point in the residence for a while.'

'I love that. It's not often that you can create such a good outcome from something so ugly.'

'Have you had any really bad situations? I guess it's different for a male, but I've heard of one or two incidents affecting males.'

'I haven't ever been attacked or anything like that – I guess I'm not outgoing enough to get myself into that sort of situation. But there are other unpleasant situations. One of the things that can happen if you're working for staffing in the university is that staff come to you confidentially to report harassment by other members of staff. I'm not a harassment contact officer, but they still seem to want to come to me because they want to make a report - contact officers are simply supposed to listen and then maybe suggest remedies, but they can't take more direct action.

'The most awful thing that happened to me was some months ago, when a junior female lecturer came to me to report that a more senior staff male was trying to force himself on her for sex, threatening to block her promotion if she didn't come across. The sort of thing that also happens with teachers and pupils, but those ones of course don't come to me.

'Anyway, this case was a very serious one, and it quite horrified me. I told the woman that I'd go immediately to more senior members of the administration and we'd get back to her. As luck would have it, the most relevant person was away, and it took me a bit longer than I'd hoped to get a response. And in that time the woman in question committed suicide – she jumped off the Marston Road railway bridge into the path of a train. You can imagine how I felt about that, being near the same spot that Rosemary was found and all. If I'd realised that she was suicidal maybe I could have stopped it, but I didn't and so that happened. I can't ever forget it. And it came back again even more horribly when I identified Rosemary Mason and heard that her body was found on the railway near the same bridge.'

'That's terrible, and I can totally understand how you feel, even though I don't think you could have anticipated the outcome. It's a good illustration of what gets called collateral damage – harm to others beyond the immediate participants. All because men wish to force themselves on to women and use their positions of power to achieve that. Like Jarrod Slater, in fact.'

'Well, you're preaching to the converted with all of this. I've never wished to do it myself – I think I've said before, in my view sex is something where the enjoyment comes from both partners wanting to do it. But maybe I'm just undersexed for a male.'

I gave him a wry look. 'Oh, I don't think I'd say that...'

I was most amused when he blushed deeply.

AGGIE RANSOME

They don't know what to do with me here now. They won't allow me out of the hospital so I can't go down to the shops any more. I used to enjoy that. I'd become quite good at shoplifting, because I knew they couldn't touch me because I was supposed to be a nutter. I knew it was wrong, but I never took anything for myself – I mostly used to take cans of cat food for the cat in our sewing room. She doesn't get much nice food otherwise, and I thought the shops could at least afford that small contribution.

What's harder is that I can't wander freely round the hospital – just to a few wards where people know me best. I used to enjoy my freedom before that.

It doesn't matter any longer, though. I've been having pains in my inside for a little while now. I haven't wanted to eat much, and I haven't been able to pass anything from my bum, so they took me to the main Infirmary for some tests. A policeman had to go with me – I don't know why. I told them I wasn't going to hurt anybody any more, but they said he still had to go. I think perhaps he just wanted to get out of the police station for a bit.

They did some tests on me, and then the main doctor told me that it wasn't good news. He said I had something growing inside me that was blocking my insides, and it was too late to do anything. He said that I could live for maybe two months more, but that might be it. He said that he could give me something to help with the pain, but I said the pain wasn't too bad at the moment and I wouldn't bother.

I asked if that nice policeman who talked to me that one day in the loony bin could come to see me once more, because I had something that I wanted to ask him. He was the only person who ever listened to me and believed what I said, and I liked him.

He came round to the hospital, and he said: 'Hello, Aggie. I hear you're not too well at the moment. I'm right sorry to hear that.'

'That's very kindly of you, but it doesn't worry me too greatly. I think I've reached the end of my time, and they won't let me do much any more. But before I go I'd like to know one thing. Can you find out for me what happened to my Uncle Bertie? Please…'

He agreed to do that, and he came back two days later.

'I've found the records. Your Uncle Bertie died twenty-four years ago. I've found the record of his death, but I haven't been able to find out where he was buried – or cremated if that's what happened.'

'Thank you for that. It doesn't really matter what happened to him – I just wanted to know that he was gone, and I don't care where his remains are now. I'd like to go and spit on his grave, but they'd never let me out of here.'

I thought for a moment longer, and then I said. 'Twenty-four years, and they never took me back home….' That really made me sad.

'I also looked up about your parents. Would you like to know?'

I just nodded.

'Your father died nineteen years ago, but your mother lived to a very old age and only died seven years ago.'

I had to think about that for a minute. Then I said: 'Thank you. You've been very kind.' I thought for a minute more, and then I said: 'I think I'll say goodbye to you now.'

'Goodbye, Aggie – and God bless you.' He sounded a bit choked up – I don't know why.

When he'd gone I thought about what he'd told me. Mum lived for all those years after Uncle Bertie and Dad had gone, and she never came to see me.

I wondered if she'd even thought about me. I'll never know.

SERGEANT NIELSEN

It took a couple of days because the lab was busy, but then we got the report back. There was no doubt at all that the bloodstains on the blanket from Mansfield Ward were from Rosemary Mason, and they were quite fresh. It seemed impossible that an outsider could have killed Rosemary in that location, and most unlikely that it was another member of the staff other than Jarrod Slater. Aggie Ransome's evidence was the clincher, though that probably wouldn't be acceptable in a court of law as she was legally regarded as a mental patient. As far as we were concerned, though, that was good confirmation.

I thought of going to tell Aggie that the tests confirmed what she'd already told us, but then I thought she'd probably take that as meaning that we didn't trust what she said. She'd had no doubt at all.

I thought I'd leave her in peace to face what she knew was coming with her cancer. She knew that she'd done something good – let her take that with her into the unknown.

I did think, though, that I might go and tell Christiane and

Philip. They didn't really need to know, but they'd tried to help as much as they could and I thought maybe I owed it to them. Besides, I've got a bit of a soft spot for yon Christiane, who's a really nice lass. If Philip has any sense at all he'll be trying to be a bit more than just her landlord. And good luck to him....

FRANK ELLIOTT

The news spread quickly round the hospital when Aggie died. There was a mixture of sadness at the fact that someone who was almost a fixture in the place wouldn't be around any more, and relief for Aggie's sake that she'd been released from what was semi-imprisonment in the hospital. Before the murder she'd been free to wander wherever she liked, and that were the only thing that made up for the fact that she were there at all. When that went she had no real life any longer.

I suppose there were one or two in the hospital – or outside it – who thought that death were only justice because she'd killed one of the nursing staff, but I couldn't have named any of them. There hadn't been much respect for Jarrod Slater, especially when people found out what he'd been doing.

The hospital couldn't find any of Aggie's family, at least none that'd own up to her, so she were quietly and privately cremated at the hospital's expense. However, a lot of people, staff and patients, felt that she deserved a small memorial service, so one were organised in the entertainment hall.

Billy Ellyard took it upon himself to set out all the chairs.

He put out every single chair that were available, and he spent every day until the service rearranging each one and lining it up carefully with the others. Some people laughed at him and said there'd never be enough people to fill half of them, but he wouldn't be budged.

The hospital chaplain agreed to arrange a simple service, roughly following a Church of England memorial service but shortened and simplified. On the day the size of the crowd was surprising, and Billy Ellyard had the last laugh. All his chairs were filled. A lot of the hospital staff came, because many of them had had a soft spot for Aggie, and most of the patients who were bright enough to know what were going on came too. My mate Len Nielsen turned up – he got on well with Aggie while he were having to question her, and I think he had a bit of a soft spot for her too. And even my mate Christina and her lad were there – I were quite touched by that.

The chaplain said a few prayers and gave a short reading, and then we all sang "All Creatures Great and Small", which were a nicer hymn than some of the ones they could have chosen. Then the chaplain said a few words about Aggie, and he did a good job in choosing the nice and the positive things that there were about her. Finally a couple more prayers and then a blessing.

I looked around the hall to see if there were anybody who might have been from Aggie's family after all, but I think I knew every face in the hall so I don't think there were any. But then again, when I looked at all the staff and the patients, and people like Len and Christina and Philip, I think perhaps her family were there after all.

A lot of family....

EPILOGUE: CHRISTIANE

I'd had an idea a little while ago, and I'd been doing a bit of research in the meantime. Way back Philip had mentioned that he and Lucy had been thinking of going to a hill tribe area in north-west Thailand, and the more I read about the various hill tribes in that region the more interesting they seemed. I wouldn't mind a visit myself as long as I had someone for company, and who better than Philip who'd already studied a lot of the background and even learnt a bit of one of the languages.

It turned out there are six main hill tribes – Lahu, Akha, Lisu, Mong or Meo, Mien or Yao, and Karen – plus quite a number of other small groups. Lisu was the tribe that Philip had said he and Lucy were planning to go to, but I read in some detail about all of the different tribes. They all sounded interesting – and probably equally challenging. I tossed up between Akha and Lisu, and in the end decided why not Lisu since Philip already had a little of the language. At least I hoped he did.

We were sitting in the kitchen one day, with the inevitable cup of coffee but no shortbread for once, when I decided to broach the subject.

'Philip, you know that you and Lucy were thinking of going to visit one of the hill tribe areas in Thailand. I'm feeling that after all this horrible business with Aggie and her tragedies, and Mr Slater, not to mention Giampaolo, I wouldn't mind a change of scenery for a little while, and something different.

'I was thinking of going myself to one of them. I've been doing a bit of investigating of the Lisu language because that's the one that you started to learn. I haven't got across the pronunciation at all yet, so I've written my question to you down.' I handed him a piece of paper that read: "*Nu ngua gel nia tit da jjei dda mat dda, Philip?*"

I wasn't totally surprised when Philip looked a bit stunned and said:

'It's kind of you to think that I might have learned a bit of the language, but I only did lesson one and that must have been at least lesson two. I'm afraid you'll have to translate it for me!'

I said: 'It means "Will you come with me, Philip?"'

An expression came over his face that was at first startled and then looked rather happy.

'Hang on a minute while I get my phrase book.' He disappeared upstairs and came back a moment later with a small booklet.

He studied it for a little while, then came back with a second piece of paper. He said: 'I'm not quite sure of this, but I think this is the answer.' The paper read: "*Lat jjei ddor wa*".

That didn't take me a lot further forward. With my heart slightly in my mouth I had to ask: 'Does that mean yes or no'?'

'I believe it means – at least it's intended to mean: 'I want to go.'

And he came over and gave me a big hug.

A very big and warm hug….

POSTSCRIPT

LUNACY IN NORTH WEST ENGLAND

Most people are frightened by madness and lunatics. But lunacy has its brighter side too – it saved employment in north-west England when cotton milling collapsed.

The north of England is well-remembered for its many mill towns – woollen mills in Yorkshire, and cotton mills in Lancashire. But when the sweatshops of the hotter colonies of Britain put the cotton mills out of business, the major employer in the north-west of England disappeared.

Its place was taken over by the health service, and within that lunacy was the biggest sector. Two large mental institutions in Lancaster served the whole of north-west England, and had more staff than any other employer.

Lancaster Moor Hospital was opened in 1816 as the County Lunatic Asylum, and it then housed just sixty patients. By the late 1940s this had grown to nearly 3,000 patients. These patients suffered from a range of psychiatric problems, rather than being mentally handicapped.

For those who were just regarded as "simple", the Royal Albert Asylum opened in 1868 when a benefactor gave a substantial donation to establish a "small asylum for idiots" on the edge of Lancaster. This also grew, and by 1978 (as the Royal Albert Hospital) it was home to 932 patients with varying degrees of mental handicap.

There were some fine examples of public benevolence in this – an embarrassing social problem solved. And one should remember that there was also self-interest here, if a family had a member that they could simply not look after. Or perhaps was just an embarrassment in front of the neighbours – the morality became a bit more doubtful there.

But there were also plenty of cases where there was no morality at all. A husband who was tiring of his wife and who had money or social influence could bribe the relevant authority to have his wife declared insane and be committed to an institution, leaving him free to carry on with his mistress.

And most cruelly of all, an uncle or a father could interfere sexually with a niece or a daughter, and then have the girl declared "morally defective" and committed to an institution, often for the remainder of her life. To be imprisoned among mental patients for the rest of your life when you yourself are totally sane is the most appalling punishment. And your only crime had been to be pretty, and to live among men who could not control their lust.

Following Care in the Community legislation in the 1980s, patients from both the Royal Albert Hospital and Lancaster Moor Hospital were relocated into the community. The Royal Albert closed in 1996, and is now the Jamea Al Kauthar Islamic College that provides Islamic education to Muslim girls. Lancaster Moor Hospital closed in 2000. Its Annexe and Chapel have been converted into apartments, and houses have been built in the hospital grounds.

AUTHOR'S STATEMENT

In this story the Royal Victoria Hospital is a thinly disguised version of the Royal Albert Hospital. I worked there for two years as pest control officer, and I have tried to be true to the physical structure and surroundings, and also to the pest controller's job.

The characters of all of the staff members are entirely fictitious, and I was not aware of any case in which a staff member interfered sexually with a patient. That was entirely for the story.

The quirks of behaviour of the patients are almost entirely real, but all of the names are fictitious. I could see no shame for anyone in including the details, and I am hoping that they will make people more sympathetic towards those who have mental problems.

Very sadly, however, my character of Aggie Ransome is based on someone who was in the hospital in my time. Like Aggie, she was only there because she had been interfered with by her uncle, and she had then been committed to the institution, I presume having been declared morally defective.

She had been there for the whole of her adult life, and she was elderly and dying of cancer just before I left. She still had fine and attractive features when I knew her, and one could see that she would have been beautiful when she was young.

Her history in that regard is similar to that of Aggie in the story, but in no other way are they the same, and the "real" Aggie most certainly did not kill anyone. My dedication of this book is to her.

It appals me that in my lifetime I could meet someone who had suffered this terrible fate. It happened in what were known as "the good old days" when I was little. The more I hear about the good old days the less I believe that they really were.

The Royal Albert had in its grounds a building with an inscription in its stone wall reading: "The Storey Home for Feeble-Minded Girls, Built by Sir Thomas Storey to Commemorate the 60th Year of Queen Victoria's Reign, 1897." One would like to think that that was just public benevolence, too.

The words and phrases in the language of the Lisu hill tribe people in NW Thailand are copied from the Thai Hill Tribes Phrasebook published by Lonely Planet (David Bradley, 1991). I don't speak the language at all, but assume that they are correct.

And a last note on the hospital. In my time there, like Philip I never managed to find out what happened to Norman's dinner either. That was a real note on a door, and my mind still boggles....

Finally, two sincere messages of thanks. Firstly to Vashti Farrer, who has encouraged my writing over the years, and who shares with me an interest in mental hospitals and the treatment of mental patients. And secondly, my heartfelt thanks to my wife Pam for putting up with my obsessive writing attempts, patiently and for so long. She shared Lancaster and the Royal Albert with me for two years, and I thank her for that too. It was located in a beautiful part of the world, and our weekends in the dales and the moors more than made up for the less happy aspects of the work.

AND A PERSONAL NOTE ON WHICH TO CONCLUDE....

I gave Christiane the surname Guchez, which was my maternal grandmother's maiden name. She was born Gabrielle Elvire Guchez to a French-speaking Belgian family in 1881, and she married a German who was manager of a large dynamite factory in Germany. At the outbreak of World War One there was great hostility between Belgium and Germany, and her Belgian family cut all ties with her for the rest of her life. I think this is very sad, though understandable, but I'd like to think that through Christiane's name at least one member of her family remembers her.

ABOUT THE AUTHOR

Paul Ferrar is a biologist who worked on dung beetles and maggots in northern Australia, and on termites in South Africa. He also worked in the Australian aid program managing co-operative research projects between Australian agricultural research scientists and those in developing countries working on similar problems.

After South Africa Paul and his wife Pam went to the United Kingdom, intending to work there for three years. Pam secured a position as a Research Assistant at Lancaster University, but a national austerity program meant that Paul was unable to find a position as a biologist. Needing a second income, he eventually took a position as Pest Control Officer at one of the two large mental hospitals in Lancaster. Well, rats, mice, ants and cockroaches are biology, after all....

They cut their stay short by a year, but the job did provide some background for this book.

The body of a young woman is found roughly buried in a remote spot in the Queensland Gulf Country. Forensic evidence from maggots in the body suggests that she must have been killed in Papua New Guinea, but the body could not possibly have moved from PNG to the Gulf within the timeline available.

Further investigation shows that she might have been caught up with drug smugglers and cattle thieves, but clues are still not forthcoming.

A maggot expert investigates in northern Cape York, aided by a young aboriginal girl who knows her country and its wildlife well. Together they try and work out what must have happened when, and who did it. They are aided by a wise hotel chambermaid, and a bird of paradise and a tree kangaroo.

www.vividpublishing.com.au/paulferrar